DATELINE: Thursday, before first bell. Day one of danc Trumbull.

SYMPTOMS OF S

GIRLS:
- Spastic hair-flipping movements
- Bursts of high-pitched, nervous giggling
- Flushed cheeks

BOYS:
- Sudden need to huddle in groups and whisper
- Inability to look any girl in the eye
- Spaced-out gaze after a pack of females cruise by
- Blushing epidemic (see "Flushed Cheeks" above)

SERIES

Girl Reporter
Snags Crush!

Created by
LINDA ELLERBEE

AVON BOOKS · NEW YORK

A Division of HarperCollinsPublishers

My deepest thanks to Katherine Drew,
Anne-Marie Cunniffe, Lori Seidner, Whitney Malone,
Roz Noonan, Alix Reid and Susan Katz, without whom
this series of books would not exist. I also want to
thank Christopher Hart, whose book *Drawing on the
Funny Side of the Brain* retaught me how to cartoon.
At age 11, I was better at it than I am now. Honest.

Drawings by Linda Ellerbee

AVON BOOKS TRADEMARK REG. U.S. PAT. OFF.
AND IN OTHER COUNTRIES, MARCA REGISTRADA, HECHO EN U.S.A.

Library of Congress Cataloging-in-Publication Data
Ellerbee, Linda.
    Girl reporter snags crush! / created by Linda Ellerbee.
        p.   cm. — (Get real ; #4)
    Summary: Intrepid eleven-year-old journalist Casey Smith protests
Crush Cola's corporate sponsorship of her school, a deal that would
give the company a monopoly on the soda sold there.
    ISBN 0-06-440758-6 (pbk.) — ISBN 0-06-028249-5- (lib. bdg.)
    [1. Corporate sponsorship—Fiction.   2. Journalism—Fiction.
3. Newspapers—Fiction.   4. Schools—Fiction]   I. Title.
PZ7.E42845 Gie 2000   99-53126
[Fic]—dc21   CIP
                                                                    AC

Typography by Carla Weise
2   3   4   5   6   7   8   9   10
❖
First Edition

For the kids,
who always get real

Strange Virus Invades Middle School

MY NAME IS Casey Smith, and I am the only sane person in my entire school.

It started this morning. It seemed like any other Thursday. I pulled on my favorite pair of perfectly broken-in blue jeans, a white T-shirt, and my red Converse hightops. Then I lugged my backpack onto my shoulder and headed out the door. Believe me, I wasn't expecting this Thursday to be anything out of the ordinary.

I mean, Trumbull Middle School isn't exactly the home of all things strange but true. As far as schools go, it's your standard mixture of beige walls and brown lockers. And Abbington, the supersleepy town where I live in the Berkshire Mountains in western Massachussetts, makes

1

everything seem so uneventful. They should rename this place Dullsville. Or Boringland. Not exactly a big humming city.

Actually, it's not even a small humming city.

At least I've got the school newspaper, *Real News*, to keep me busy. It's true that I have to keep my reporter's radar on overdrive to find anything juicy, but I do manage to write up some hard-hitting stories when it really counts.

Most of the time.

There has been the occasional issue where my name didn't appear on the front page. But it wasn't my fault. I blame those practically un-readable issues on our editor in chief, Megan O'Connor, better known as the Princess of Pink, or the Sugarplum Fairy, or (fill in your favorite gooey word here). She and I have very different ideas about what makes good news.

My ideas: environmental pollution, child abuse, crooked community leaders. *Real* news. News that matters. Megan's ideas: school plays, parades, cheerleading tryouts.

With that mentality, why not just write about this week's beefaroni special in the school cafeteria?

PARENTS PROTEST BARFARONI HOT LUNCH!
Hundreds of Kids Hurl Through Night Following Trumbull Meal!

Do I sound like I'm on my reporter's soapbox? It happens. Megan gets under my freckled skin like no one else.

But more on Megan later. As I said, it started out a normal morning. I walked the last few blocks to school, passing more and more kids. Just like always.

But they were acting strange.

Take Gary Williams, for example. Gary's the sports reporter for *Real News*. He's a jock, fine, but he also has a pretty sharp brain. Usually.

But today, Gary was low on gray matter. Actually, pink matter was flying over his head. He was holding up a neon-purple notebook, sassing some girl. His baby dreadlocks swayed, and his brown lips were curved in a goofy grin. Then he took off running.

"Coming through!" Gary hollered, nearly knocking me out of my hightops. He bolted past me and across the school lawn. That's when I noticed the pink flamingos on his notebook. Correction: it was definitely not his notebook.

"Hey, what's up with—?"

I was interrupted by a high-pitched shriek. It was followed by a wind-rush of perfume that belonged to Janelle Watson. She raced past me, chasing Gary. Obviously trying to get her flamingos back.

Gary stopped running and hoisted the notebook again. Janelle jumped up and down, giggling and reaching. Finally she kicked him in the shins. He dropped the notebook. She picked it up. And the chase continued.

What are we, in second grade?

I kept walking. Maybe I needed breakfast or something.

Then I saw Ringo, who is easy to spot. Think purple socks, tie-dyed shirts and sandals. Ringo's my bud and the *Real News* resident cartoonist. He's also my best friend at Trumbull since my old best friend, Griffin, moved to Baltimore.

Some kids just don't get Ringo. Maybe because he's the only boy cheerleader at school. That's right. A boy rah-rah. But I love him for his Planet Ringo way of seeing stuff. You tell him the sky is blue, and he'll go on a philosophical rant about how you don't know what blue *really* is. As soon as you think you've got Ringo figured out, he'll pull a doozy on you.

Like right now.

Ringo was doing some over-the-top hip-hop dance moves near the school entrance. His arms were wheeling around like he was about to take flight. His legs looked disconnected from the rest of him, bouncing up and down like they were made of rubber.

At first I thought maybe the cheerleaders were having a practice. But Ringo was the only one dancing. The other rah-rahs were just watching and clapping.

Then it hit me: Ringo was showing off. For a group of girls.

What was going on? That was two weirdnesses in two minutes. Was there something in the air?

I escaped into the staleness of corridor city, where I spotted Megan at her locker. Probably lining up pink notebooks beside matching pencils. Which would go with today's outfit: pink sweater set, khaki pants, pale-pink socks and polished penny loafers.

"What's up, Megan?" I said. "No, let me guess. You're lining your locker in strawberry-scented paper?" I pulled my backpack off my shoulders and balanced it on my sneakers.

"Do they have strawberry-scented paper?" she said, perky as a poodle. My jokes tend to go right over Megan's hairspray-scented head.

"Have you noticed anything strange?" I asked, pulling out my trusty reporter's notebook.

She stopped to adjust the glitter butterfly pin in her blond hair. "Strange how?"

"I'm not sure yet." I glanced around me. "But look at that group of guys." I pointed down the hall. "Usually, they look like they're waiting to be introduced to Mr. Comb and Ms. Brush. Now they've got their hair plastered down with gel. I'm baffled."

Megan glanced over and shrugged. "Well, this is just a guess," she said. "But maybe they're trying to look good so they can ask someone to the school dance next Friday. They've only got a week left."

School dance? I practically laughed out loud. All this trouble for a stupid dance? I didn't even bother to write this down.

Satisfied and ready to leave Megan to her pinkness, I started to put my notebook away when Gary and Ringo cruised up with our *Real News* staff photographer, Toni Velez. Usually we meet in the *Real News* office for morning meetings, but this was as good as anywhere, I guess.

"I can't believe that guy Ernie," Toni said as she dumped her bag on the ground. "He just asked me to the dance, but I already know he asked my friend Tanya. Which means I was his second choice. I told him to take a hike."

That's Toni. She's got as much attitude as she does thick, curly hair. Boom-chicka-boom, Gram calls it. Which can be a good thing . . . or a dangerous thing. I guess it depends what side of the "boom" you're on.

One thing's for sure. Whoever Ernie is, he's doomed.

"So who do you want to go with?" Megan asked Toni brightly.

"I don't know," she answered, tucking a strand of orange-streaked hair behind her ear. "But I'm sick of waiting around for a guy to ask. Like I have time for this?"

"Excuse me?" I cut in. "Toni Velez, waiting for a guy? Don't tell me you're afraid to ask some boy to the dance."

"She can't. Not for this dance," Megan said. "Guys ask girls to the first dance of the year. It's tradition."

I rolled my eyes. How did Megan know all these useless rules and traditions?

"Maybe I'll just go with a group of girls," Toni said. There was a certain dare in her amber eyes.

"With a group?" Gary chimed in. "No way. You can't do that." He turned to Megan. "Can she?"

"A lot of people are doing the group thing," Megan said. "Do you know what you're going to wear, Toni? I'm thinking about my—"

"Enough!" I jerked my pack onto my shoulder. "You guys are making my head hurt."

All four of them stared at me.

"You're not *all* planning on going to this dumb dance, are you? Ringo?" I asked, with my eyebrows raised practically to my hairline.

"Right! If we're all going, we can carpool.

Who's mom has the biggest car?" Ringo asked, missing my point.

"Reeen-gooo, you *know* what I mean," I said, clenching my teeth together tightly. "I can't believe this wannabe boogiefest is so important to everyone."

"Casey," Megan said, her face one big princess frown. "Leave it to you to be crabby about a dance. Can't you have any fun?"

I pictured Megan forcing me to dress up in an itchy dress and wear ugly baby's breath flowers in my hair just so I could be bored out of my skull.

I mean, it's a dance. Whoop-dee-doo.

A bunch of kids who see each other all day in school take a perfectly good night out of their weekend to go back to their same school and stand in the same gym where they usually fling volleyballs. And somehow, because it's decorated to look like Tahiti or Paris, it's supposed to be this big thrill.

Get real.

"Fun?" I squinted at Megan. "If your idea of fun is doing the Electric Slide with your lab partner from science, then count me out."

"The dance is a super idea for the school," Megan said like a spokesmodel. "It's a way for people to meet even if they don't have a class together. To loosen up and forget about grades and tests for one night."

While Megan yammered on about the social benefits of a dance, I sank down to the ground. Resting against a locker, I slowly banged the back of my head against the metal.

Thunk. Thunk. Thunk.

"I can't wait to bust a move on the dance floor." Ringo did a move that made his head look disconnected from his shoulders.

I zoned out and opened my reporter's notebook, which is totally flamingo-free, thank you very much. I looked around me at the other kids in the hall. I could be wrong, but I had the feeling the dance was the topic of every conversation. Maybe I should write this down. I started scribbling:

DATELINE: Thursday, before first bell.
Day one of dance craziness infecting
Trumbull.
SYMPTOMS OF STRANGE BEHAVIOR:
  GIRLS:
  • Spastic hair-flipping movements
  • Bursts of high-pitched, nervous
    giggling

- Flushed cheeks

BOYS:
- Sudden need to huddle in groups and whisper
- Inability to look any girl in the eye
- Spaced-out gaze after a pack of females cruise by
- Blushing epidemic (see "Flushed Cheeks" above)

I studied the list, then looked at the goofiness of the people all around me. It was as if the kids at my school had been kidnapped by space aliens and replaced with glassy-eyed disco divas.

Or maybe there was another explanation.

CONCLUSION: A rampant case of First Dance Flu!!!

Reporters Mud Wrestle on School Lawn!

THAT WAS IT. Some airborne dance virus had infected the middle school halls, making kids mucho loco.

I was ready to give my friends a shot of reality. Time to tell them they were all actually very sick, and that I'd work on a remedy to cure them. But just as I opened my mouth, Tyler McKenzie joined the circle.

Gulp.

"Hey guys, what's up?" he said, all smooth and cool.

I was staring at the smashed thumbnail on his right hand. Then I noticed how his caramel-brown hair was the exact color of his eyes, which were the exact color of my freckles. And just as I was about to jump up and say hi, he turned toward Megan.

"I had this awesome idea for a story," he said, shifting his backpack from his left shoulder to his right. "I know I'm not a reporter or anything. . . ."

"Hit me," Megan said.

Ringo slapped her shoulder.

"Funny, Ringo." Megan turned back to Tyler. "You don't have to be on staff to write a story. What's the idea?"

"Do you know what off-road biking is?"

Gary perked up. "Isn't that where guys get on mountain bikes and go zooming down the sides of hills and through dirt and rivers and stuff?"

"Guys and girls," Tyler explained. "But there's a lot more to it than that. I went to an exhibition last week, and it was killer. The bikes are completely high-tech. And you don't even have to be on a team to do it. There were tons of kids out there. Turns out Abbington is a great place for this sport."

"Because it's all hilly with grooves," Ringo said. "Hilly and groovy. Groovy Hills."

"Uh, yeah," Tyler said, looking at Ringo, sort of confused. A lot of people look at Ringo that way. "I got so psyched about it, I just wrote this story for your paper."

Her paper? That hurt.

"Wow, fabulous!" Megan said, flipping into editor mode as easily as she flips her hair. "I'll read it today. I'm thinking that a list of hot spots in Abbington would be a terrif sidebar."

"Is that like a handlebar?" Ringo asked, completely serious.

"No, a sidebar can be a list of practical information that goes along with a more general story," Megan informed him.

I knew that. But I wasn't into showing off my journalism knowledge. Not like some people I know.

"Why don't you do a handlebar sidebar?" Ringo asked.

Gary knocked on Ringo's forehead. Megan just sighed. I was enjoying myself. At least they weren't talking about the stupid dance anymore.

Then Tyler turned to me. "Hey, Casey, why are you camping out on the ground?" My stomach flipped and flopped. I think my guts were having their own dance.

"Oh, me? This? I'm just, you know, just . . . resting . . . I guess." That's the kind of brilliant repartee that makes a good reporter stand out.

"What's up?" he asked, holding out his hand to help me up.

I didn't take it. But I stood up anyway and smoothed my jeans with my palms. I tucked my hair behind my ears and finally stuck my hands in my jean pockets like I was trying to stretch them out.

"What's up?" I repeated. "Isn't it obvious? This whole school is lacking in intelligent life! I mean, you'd think Madonna was visiting next Friday. Can you believe how everybody's walking around like dance-crazed cuckoos?"

"I guess," he said. But he didn't sound convinced.

"I've decided it's an epidemic," I went on, unable to stop myself. "The First Dance Flu. People are dropping like flies—or like butterfly hair clips."

"Uh-huh," Tyler said. He was stepping backward a little.

Maybe I haven't mentioned that I have a tendency to rant about things I really care about? Or in this case, really *don't* care about. But why was I blabbering to Tyler? Why couldn't I just say "Hello, how's it going?" like everybody else? Why did I have to go on and on and on and . . .

"I used to think the kids here were relatively normal," I heard myself continue. "But this dance fever business has me questioning everybody's sanity." The only thing missing from my speech was a big fist in the air.

"Yeah, okay, Casey." Tyler shifted from his left foot to his right. "I hope you find the cure for the flu or whatever."

14

I stood there, feeling like an idiot.

"I'll let you know about your story," Megan blurted, and for once I was relieved she piped up.

"'Bye, guys." Within seconds, Tyler was part of the blur of kids herding down the hall to their first class.

"I think he's done bumming on you for the factory fiasco," Ringo said.

Back in September, I did a *Real News* story that closed down a factory and sort of got Tyler's father fired from his job. It wasn't a pretty picture. Tyler hated me for a while. And who could blame him?

"Yeah," Toni jumped in. "I think he's way over being mad."

"That'd be nice," I said, thinking out loud. "He's nice. I mean, in general. Generally nice. At least, not mean. I mean, niceness is a long way from forgiveness."

I felt my face get hot. Megan and Ringo exchanged a knowing glance. What was that about? I didn't like Tyler. At least, not Dance Flu like him. Why were they exchanging knowing glances? I hate knowing glances that I'm not a part of because that means the people glancing are knowing something about me.

"Don't get any cute ideas into your cute little heads," I said. "I'm not glopping on lip gloss for

Tyler between tardy bells."

"Casey, if you like him, a little lip gloss might be just what you need," Megan said, in that here's-some-friendly-advice voice that drives me absolutely bonkers. Was this middle school or the makeover channel?

"Megan, did you forget your reality pills today?" I asked, putting my hand on her shoulder like a good doctor. "On Planet Earth, some girls don't live for makeup and dances and scented stationery—"

"Excuse me," a voice grumbled loudly behind me.

I turned around and saw a big man wheeling a hulking soft-drink machine down the hall on one of those dollies. I stepped out of his way, but I was pretty sure he would've run me over if I hadn't.

"Hey, watch it!" I said, as he hauled the machine past me, practically smashing my toes. Two other guys, each carting a machine, were smack behind him, and all five of us had to back up against the lockers.

My reporter radar started tingling. *This* was almost as unusual as Dance Flu behavior.

I followed the convoy of men to the door, waving at my friends to come along. The men carted every soda machine down to a big white truck at the curb. Other workmen were lifting big boxes of soda out of a second truck and carrying them into the school. Were they replacing the old soda? And why?

My nose twitched. That meant possible story.

"What's with the big soda exchange? I smell a story," I said.

Ringo breathed in deeply. "Hmm. All I smell are hash browns from the cafeteria. I'd exchange soda for some hash browns right now."

"All I smell is a reporter trying to change the subject," Megan said. "Men replacing old soda machines is not spine-tingling stuff."

And the dance is? "Megan, duh! *All* the machines? Broken at the same time?" I asked.

"Speaking of broken," Megan said, ignoring me. "Did you break that story on the science labs yet? The final draft is due tomorrow, you know."

"Yes, Megan. I'm aware of that," I said crisply. "And yes, you'll have it right on time."

"Great," she said, not registering my 'tude. "You did use the same basic idea as the first draft you gave me, right?"

"Right," I told her, yanking my gaze away from the soda mafia in the truck. This was a strange place for a *Real News* staff meeting, but I can talk about news anytime. "Same angle. The science labs in this school are seriously strapped for cash—unlike the sports teams. Speaking of which,

I hope we're putting this story on the front page, instead of that football puff piece that Gary's working on."

"Excuse me?" Gary objected. "Conway is the best linebacker we've had since the last time we took the division title. That's big news, man."

"Uh-huh. And what does a linebacker do, exactly? Except for eat more food than Godzilla and bump into other guys for a trophy."

Gary said: "He takes up the whole front page."

Toni snickered. I pinged Gary on the shoulder.

"Why don't you get the story in first?" Megan suggested. "Then we'll talk about who gets the front page."

Bleah.

The truth was, I wasn't too psyched about this science story. It was better than nothing—and way better than some football story. But it wasn't the kind of groundbreaking, earthshaking, attention-grabbing story I crave.

I mean, underfunded science labs? I can see the headlines now:

SCIENCE LABS ABANDONED!
Dead Frogs Stinking Up School Flower Beds!

"I just need a little more background," I told Megan. "I'm covering the student government meeting today after school. But I'll rewrite the science lab story tonight."

"Super!" Megan said. Can you stand it? She's so sugary, you can feel a zit forming as she speaks. "I'll see you at the meeting."

Megan at the meeting? "Wait, are you covering the meeting?" I asked. The SGA meetings are a step above math homework. I didn't want to go if I didn't have to.

"No, I'm not," she said, suddenly losing her Madame Editor focus. "I mean . . . Oh! Well, I'm going, but I just thought I'd . . ." Megan's voice trailed off. She isn't exactly a bucket of laughs, but usually Megan can finish a sentence.

"So, yeah, I'll see you there," Megan said, straightening her sweater with one hand as she flipped her hair back with the other. I couldn't tell if she was suddenly nervous, embarrassed, distracted, or just really, really coordinated.

My nose twitched again. Megan had no business at an SGA meeting. Did she know something I didn't? Could the soda machine guys have anything to do with this? And why was she suddenly so tongue-tied?

I definitely smelled a story.

Or was I just getting a cold?

Principal Without Principle
Puts School on Auction Block!

I KNOW IT seems like a nutty thing to be thinking about. Soda machines aren't exactly thrilling. And even if there was a story, it would be about carbonated sugar water. Who ever heard of a front-page story about bubbly corn syrup?

But something was nagging at me about those trucks and those guys carting cases of soda into the school. The science lab story wasn't done, but I couldn't concentrate on that until I nosed around this soda situation.

I forced myself to focus on morning classes. When gym was finally over, I threw on my clothes and blew out of the locker room. I wanted to check the vending machine area in the cafeteria. Maybe talk to Mrs. Stekol, the lunch lady at Trumbull. She actually wears one of those freaky

"ODE TO A SODA"

You made me put
The coins in first.
But after that
You chilled my thirst.
Is this the last
Sweet sugar blast?
So long, soft drink
Gone in a blink.
Rock on always!
Effervesce new hallways!

hair nets, but I think that's part of the health code.

When the bell rang, I bolted out the door like an escapee and headed to the lunchroom. The vending area was empty. No machines at all, just dusty outlines of the old ones.

Mrs. Stekol was placing the large metal trays of pasta and burgers and other curious foodstuffs into the bins, getting ready for the first lunch rush.

"Hello, Mrs. Stekol," I called out.

"Yes, yes, who is . . . ?" she asked. "Oh my! If it is not my favorite reporter, Barbara Walters!"

Never mind that Babs isn't exactly my speed. I'm into real news, not celebrity interviews. But I needed info, so I pushed on.

"Mrs. Stekol, do you have any idea what happened to the soda machines?" I asked.

"You are growing girl, Casey," she said. "You should not drink such sugar." She plucked a carton of milk from the bin and handed it to me. "Take this now and you can pay me next week."

That was Mrs. Stekol. You could always count on her if you forgot your lunch. But lunch was for later. At the moment I had a few cartons of soda to track down. "So you don't know where all the machines went?"

"I know nothing of soda machines coming or going. My apology, Casey. You are hungry?"

I eyed the piles of food in front of her. Why is it that no matter what's cooking, the cafeteria always smells the same? Sort of a cross between a wet rug and stale popcorn.

"Thanks, but no thanks," I said. "I'd rather eat real food. I mean, good food. I mean—"

She waved a wobbly stalk of celery at me. "We have plenty of the good food here."

"Right, but I packed a lunch," I said. Kids were starting to line up behind me, so I ducked out of the line and whipped out my notebook.

DATELINE: Thursday, free period

Soda machine mystery

Where did old machines go?

Where have boxes of soda from truck
been stored?

CLUES: Zilch

INTERVIEWS: Mrs. Stekol: Zilch

I had lots of questions. Not lots of answers.

I tapped my pen on the page and zoned out on a fresh glittery dance poster plastered on the wall in front of me. When do these people find time for painting posters *and* sprinkling glitter on them?

And ooh, speaking of time, I realized I only had twenty more minutes to hit the science labs and finish researching my story.

I swung by Ms. Branston's biology class and was hit by that sour-vinegar science smell the second I opened the door. Nasty!

I saw clusters of kids crowding around the green-topped counters. Counters that had rusty spigots on the top. Two walls were lined with shelves that were nearly empty. A half-empty rack of test tubes and a few petri dishes sat there, collecting dust.

I introduced myself. Ms. Branston nodded, looking strained. Like an invisible elf was sitting on her shoulders and pulling her hair out, one strand at a time.

"There's not a lot to show you," she said, waving a hand around at the classroom like a model in a furniture showroom. "Look at this. At any given moment, half the students are sitting around doing nothing. I've got four kids sharing one antique microscope. It's impossible to get anything done."

I had to admit it did look a little hopeless. "What about those things on top of the table?" I asked. "What's that equipment for?"

"They used to be gas spigots we used for various experiments," she said. "But the gas lines are old. They could leak. We had to shut them off last year because they're a fire hazard. Now we just read about those experiments instead of actually performing them."

Gas leaks? Fires? Kids reading about experiments instead of doing them? Or worse, kids doing nothing in class? I was scribbling in my notebook wildly. This was a good story after all. I felt my heart rate increase. Journalism rocks.

"Do you like science, Casey?" Ms. Branson asked me.

That's like asking a kid if she likes skinned knees.

Before I could answer, she went on. "I know some kids think it's boring because there's reading involved. But if I could hand kids some beakers and microscopes, they could strap on goggles and really get in there and experiment. Science in action. Hands-on experiments are what it's all about."

Scoop! There's my quote! I pictured kids in white lab coats transferring blue liquid from one glass container to another, curiously inspecting a smoking pot on a Bunsen burner. She was right. Science could be fun if you got to *do* science. Even growing mold in the third grade was pretty cool. Every day there was a little more green fuzz.

I thanked Ms. Branston, then bailed before the smell of formaldehyde could curl my hair.

I cruised through the rest of the day. Sure, visions of the soda police still danced in my head. But for the moment, that story was on hold. Next on my list: the boring old student government.

When the last bell rang I left Spanish class, dumped some unnecessary stuff in my locker and headed off to the meeting. I spotted Megan just outside the auditorium, checking her face in a small mirror.

"Mirror, mirror in your hand, who's the vainest in the land?" I singsonged. "Is that lip gloss, or have you been drinking canola oil out of the bottle?"

She cut me a hostile look. But before she could say anything, Ms. Nachman, the principal, went past us into the auditorium.

That was odd. SGA meetings are a snooze, and the principal never attends. The vice principal usually comes, but even he looks like he'd rather be cleaning out his garage. Now I had Megan *and* Ms. Nachman at this meeting?

My news nose was on fire.

"Come on, Glamour Gal." I pulled on Megan's elbow. "Let's go get a seat and see why Nachman herself is gracing us with her presence."

We walked into the room as Spencer Woodham, the president of the SGA, called the meeting to order. He's a very high-profile eighth grader who's always got a flock of chicks on his tail. Megan and I found two seats near the back of the room on the center aisle.

"Now, we have some important things to discuss," Spencer said. "For this week's meeting, I move that we forgo parlimentary procedure and go right into new business. All those in favor, say

'Aye.'" Ayes rang out from several places. "Great. I think we all know Ms. Nachman." With that, he flashed a toothy grin and stepped aside to let her approach the podium.

"I've got an exciting announcement," Ms. Nachman said in her trumpety politician voice. Smoothing her suit against her sides, she went on: "Something wonderful has happened that is going to be of enormous help to Trumbull Middle School. As you all know, certain departments are experiencing difficulties from lack of funding."

That was for sure. I'd seen one of those departments today.

"I've made arrangements to end all of that. With our new school sponsor, we'll soon have new uniforms for the sports teams, a face-lift renovation for the school auditorium, lab equipment for the science classes, and much, much more."

Whoa. What was this? I mean, it was news. But what was it? Suddenly my hot science lab story was about as cold as those out-of-use gas lines. I knew a sponsor was someone or something that contributed money to an organization, be it a school or a ballpark or a theater. But who was this sponsor? An eccentric billionaire? A famous graduate of Trumbull? I seriously doubted someone would just give us a big chunk of change because we were all so cute. Speaking of cute, I glanced at Megan, who looked like her brain was spinning as fast as mine.

"I suppose you're all wondering where the money is coming from," continued Ms. Nachman.

Well, duh.

"The donation amounts to a corporate sponsorship," Ms. Nachman explained. "Crush Cola has agreed to donate money to our school. In return, we've agreed to let them sell their product on our campus—*exclusively*. Starting next week, Crush Cola will be the official drink of Trumbull students."

Kids started whispering and giggling, but Ms. Nachman shushed them.

"We'll also put their logo on the athletic field's scoreboard, and on our team uniforms. The logo will appear on the sides of five school buses, as well. That'll brighten things up, won't it?" she chirped.

"It sure will," Spencer said, standing up and starting to clap. "I think this is an incredible opportunity for Trumbull." Most students in the room followed his lead and started clapping like trained seals.

Was I the only person who'd actually heard what Ms. Nachman had said? Did these robots get that their school had just got sold out big-time? Did it go over everyone's head but mine that our school would sell *only* Crush soda? As in a monopoly.

Plus the ads. At school. On jerseys and buses. This was a capitalist marketing nightmare. And it was happening at our school.

I turned to Megan and was totally shocked to see her clapping too. I mean, I didn't expect a lot from Megan, but I expected more than this.

"Um, excuse me?" I said loudly, raising my hand and standing. My notebook clattered to the floor.

"The floor recognizes, uh . . ." Spencer didn't know me. Since he was an eighth grader he didn't have much time for us lowly sixth-grade grommets. And the fact that I was on the school newspaper didn't matter. Megan and I had to re-start *Real News* because years ago students had abandoned it. And some of the older kids still rolled their eyes at the newspaper.

Well, no matter. Spencer was about to come face-to-face with Casey Smith, take-no-prisoners girl reporter.

"Casey Smith." I finished his sentence for him and took a deep breath. "Ms. Nachman, I'm aware that this school needs cash really badly. In fact, I just spent the day researching a story for *Real News* on lousy lab equipment. But don't you think the students should have a say in a decision like this? This Crush thing is going to be in their faces every day. Going to school. During school. And after school at games and stuff. Why is this the first we're hearing of it?"

Smoothing her suit a second time, Ms. Nachman answered: "I don't see how anyone could possibly object." She looked like she'd love to stick my head in her file cabinet under "SU" for Shut Up.

"I'm not saying we object," I said, noticing that there were a lot of eyes staring my way. "I'm just saying we should be consulted. And another thing, what gives this company the right to have a monopoly at our school?"

"Well, it's not a monopoly," Ms. Nachman said tersely. "They're paying for the right to sell their product here. Paying money we desperately need. All students are, of course, free to bring in other soda if they like. But on this campus, we'll only sell Cru—"

"And since when do we allow advertising on school property?" I interrupted.

Ms. Nachman paused with her mouth open.

"I mean, what comes next? Is our school going to be one big billboard? Will our textbooks have hidden messages making us want to buy a certain brand of pencils and paper? Are we going to pick up our copies of *Huck Finn* and find him drinking

Crush Cola at the end of chapter seven?"

Have I mentioned that I get a little heated? That's me, melodramatic motormouth. I try to put my brain in gear before my tongue hits the gas, but most of the time my reporter instincts are on autopilot. It isn't a bad thing, when the timing's right. Of course, when the timing is wrong, I get a lot of dirty looks. Like now.

"Casey," Ms. Nachman said, in the same tone of voice that a homeowner might use to say "termites." "Nobody is making the school into a billboard. We're just talking about a few posters here and there. You kids wear T-shirts with logos for teams or designers all the time. It's really the same thing."

I heard a few murmurs of agreement from the kids on the SGA.

"Oh, please!" I scowled. I was nothing if not eloquent.

"I would suggest," she said, her tone growing icicles, "that you think of the good of the whole school."

I wasn't backing down. "I believe that's what I'm doing," I said, folding my arms across my chest. Nothing gets my blood boiling more than a grown-up who treats me like a know-nothing kid. I was only eleven, but excuse me for knowing the difference between a logo and a conspiracy.

"Ms. Nachman?" a member of the SGA said mousily, raising her hand slowly like her arm was paining her. "I was just thinking. . . ."

Beginner's luck.

"Like, Casey has a point . . . I think," she ventured.

Had I judged this girl too quickly?

"Like, I don't really like cola because it has caffeine and sugar," she said timidly. "But if Crush Cola is the only drink sold in school, I'm going to be out of luck."

There was a jangling sound. I turned to see a girl in the last row with her hand raised. A hand with about a hundred silver rings on it. "I really don't think we should be encouraging kids to drink soda at all," she said. "It's not healthy, and I've been trying to get juice into those soda machines for a year now."

"Yes, April, I'm aware of your campaign," Ms. Nachman said through gritted teeth. The noise level in the room rose as people began muttering to each other. Reactions. Opinions.

So maybe every SGA meeting wasn't boring after all.

Ms. Nachman raised her voice. "Please, everyone. Try to keep in mind that if you want the school to have any kind of extracurriculars, we're going to have to make some compromises."

"Hey, guys!" Spencer banged his gavel on the podium. "I'm sure we've all got questions for Ms. Nachman on this issue. But no matter what, we all agree that we want the best for the school, right?"

The muttering subsided a little, and he flashed that charming grin again. Politicians. The right words, the right smile, the wrong motives.

Spencer said something about discussing it further at another meeting. "But what if that's too late?" I called out.

"Casey, thanks very much for your comments." Spencer pointed his gavel at me with a look that said "Cork it, girl!" Then he rolled right into a roundup of the old business from last week's meeting and the new items on the agenda. I had no choice but to sit back down.

Also, Megan was tugging so hard on the hem of my sweatshirt, I thought she was going to rip it.

"All right, already," I griped. I slumped into my folding chair and fished my notebook from the floor. "Don't have twenty-pound twins over this, Megan. I'm finished."

"You'd better be," Megan whispered back angrily. Jeez, she was sure fired up.

"What's wrong?" I said while I dug around in my backpack.

"*You* are wrong!" she insisted. "How could you openly oppose the student government like that?"

"I *thought* I was challenging Ms. Nachman's dictatorship," I said, enjoying the little vein above her perfect left eyebrow. It pops out when she's mad. I seem to be the person who pushes that pop-out button the most. "And since when are you the SGA's public defender?"

"Just forget it, Casey!" She crossed her legs and folded her arms and shut me out. She stared at the podium for the rest of the meeting. You'd think Spencer was revealing tomorrow's winning lottery numbers. I guess I really got under her glitter-painted nails. And I still didn't know why she was there.

Well, that wasn't important right now. What mattered was that I had another story to investigate. Forget the science lab story. Forget the stupid dance. Forget Megan's mystery visit to the SGA meeting.

I had to find out the real deal behind truckloads of soda translating to truckloads of money.

Frankly, the whole thing was making me thirsty.

Reporter Lost in Outer Space! No One Hears Her Scream!

To: Thebeast
From: Wordpainter
AM I ALONE IN THE UNIVERSE? CAN NO-
BODY HEAR ME SCREAMING? IS ADVERTISING
IN SCHOOL SOMETHING TO JUST IGNORE
BECAUSE THE GYM NEEDS A COAT OF PAINT?
TELL ME I'M NOT LOST IN SPACE!

I hit Send and my words popped up in the
Instant Message screen, highlighted in red.

I leaned back in my chair and looked around
my bedroom. It's the place to be when I've got a
lot on my mind. I fiddled with the little trouble
dolls my mom had sent me from Guatemala and
waited for Griffin's reply.

To: Wordpainter
From: Thebeast
     I'm not sure I hear you screaming. But I can see you typing. You are not lost in space! But would you please hit the Caps Lock button? I'm getting a headache.

I typed a lowercased "sorry" and hit Send. Luckily, Griffin understands that I have the patience of a toddler who's just downed a whole can of . . . Crush Cola.

I loved these chats with Griffin. Ever since he packed up with his parents and moved to Baltimore at the end of last year, these daily cyber sessions had been like breathing for me. You can't just cut yourself off cold turkey from your best friend from kindergarten. And besides, Griffin knows the real me. No smokescreens. Ever.

Rubbing my Tibetan riverstones in my hand, I thought of how to explain the whole Crush mess to Griffin. If the SGA meeting wasn't bad enough, there was also the spat between Megan and me after the meeting was over.

Basically, I told her I was going to bury Spencer Woodham for kissing up to the administration in my write-up of the meeting.

"He is *not* kissing up!" she insisted. "And keep

in mind that you're writing an article, not an editorial. Don't add your opinion. Just the facts."

"And when do I get to state my case?" I asked her.

"That's between Mr. Baxter and me," she said defiantly, sniffing. "As editor in chief, it's up to me and our advisor to make the call as to whether *Real News* should take a position on this issue."

I hate it when Megan pulls editor rank on me. "Oh, great!" I threw my hands in the air. "Leaving you and a teacher in charge? We might as well write stories about how kids who eat veggies score higher on tests."

My fingers typed furiously as I recounted my conversation for Griffin. She was going to censor me, shut me up.

But she had saved her real ammunition for last.

"Why do you have to make trouble over something good?" Megan said, waving a green photocopied piece of paper in my face. "When I say this deal is good for the students, I mean *all* the students. Including the staff of *Real News*."

"What's that?" I asked, trying to read the flapping piece of paper.

It was a list of all the activities and departments that would get funding from the Crush deal. And *Real News* was on the list.

We were supposed to get new computers and scanners.

Did I explain that the *Real News* staff has to work in a tiny closet on old computers with faulty software? You can practically see a squirrel running behind every screen. Better computers would mean a better newspaper.

As I hammered away at my message to Griffin, I had a vision of a new newspaper office. Big windows. Shiny new computers with color printers and high-speed links to the web. It would be a dream come true.

But was it worth the price?

It took me so long to explain about the whole Crush craziness that my hands were throbbing when I was finally ready to send the message.

While I waited for his reply, I kicked my Converses off and stuffed my stinky socks inside the shoes. Then the message blinked up on my screen.

To: Wordpainter
From: Thebeast
   I agree with you. Definitely. This is a hot-button issue. I bet you knocked on plenty of people's noggins about advertising in school. But what's keeping you

from spreading the word in the usual Casey Smith way?

Do I smell . . . fear?

I shivered. Sometimes Griffin knows what I'm feeling before I can nail it down myself.

I e-mailed back that I was afraid. Though I wasn't sure why. Then I told him about the dance dorkazoids, and the Tyler thing in the hall, and all the hair gel and stuff.

To: Wordpainter
From: Thebeast

Are you sure this is Casey Smith I'm talking to? Casey . . . have you been abducted by aliens, too? When are you going to fess up to this thing with Tyler? And why are you bumming on a dance? People love that stuff. I gotta say it again: RE-LAX!

Yeah, yeah, yeah. Everyone seems to think going to a dance is this completely normal activity. I am not kidding when I say that going to the dentist sounded better to me.

I e-mailed good night to Griffin, but I was still restless.

I had just chucked my Indonesian hand puppets across the room when Gram peeked her head in.

Gram is taking care of me while my parents are away on their latest Doctors Without Borders trip. My big brother, Billy, is with them. They travel all over the world and help people who can't afford health care where they need it most—like at nuclear spills or where a hurricane or an epidemic devastates a community or even a whole country. That's why I have all this groovy stuff, like my Chinese pillows and trouble dolls, around my room.

Gram stays with me while they're off doing their good deeds, which is completely awesome because for one thing, she's great. But also because she was this big deal award-winning journalist in New York and is teaching me everything she knows about being a reporter.

"Casey, my love, why are you abusing those poor puppets?" she asked, tying her bathrobe around her T-shirt. She wears this red silk bathrobe whenever she works. She must have been working on her book—it's her memoirs of being a journalist on Capitol Hill.

"I'm just stressed over this Crush thing," I answered sulkily. I'd already filled Gram in on the soda details over dinner. Sausage pizza with olives, hold the Crush Cola.

"Having second thoughts?" she asked, folding her arms.

"No way!" I insisted. "I'm just . . . over-whelmed." I held up the tiniest trouble doll. "This is me." Then I hoisted a statue of an elephant. "And this is Crush Cola. Do I stand a chance?"

"Maybe not in a battle of force. But when it comes to matching wits?" Gram smiled at me with that sweet face grandparents save just for their grandkids. "My money's on you."

Grunting, I lowered the elephant statue onto the bottom shelf. Then I did some air punches over it. "Gram? When you were tracking down sources and politicians, were you ever scared?"

"Out of my wits, sometimes," she said emphatically. "Once I got so nervous, I lost my voice. Told the source it was laryngitis. Got the sympathy interview."

I smiled.

"But fear is normal. Don't you think every last person who stands up for what she believes in gets scared on occasion?"

I hadn't thought about it that way.

She blew me a kiss and pointed at her watch. I guessed it was pretty late. I pulled my legs into my chest and rested my chin on my knees.

Gram was right. I could stand up to Crush Cola and their flashy cash. Even if it did mean sacrificing new computers for *Real News*.

Then I had another awful thought.

If Crush won and they gave us new computers, would they want something from us in return? Like, what if Crush Cola wanted us to put their logo on the masthead of our newspaper? If it was so easy for Ms. Nachman to hand over our sports teams and buses to this corporation, what would stop her from agreeing to sell out the newspaper for a few more bleachers on the back baseball diamond? Or new couches for the teacher's lounge? Or, or, or . . .

I'd had enough worrying for one night. I washed up and pulled on a big old T-shirt. Then I pounced on my bed and hugged my pillow as tight as I could. The moon was barely glowing through my window in a soft shaft of light. I took a deep breath and tried to close my eyes, but they pulled open as if they had a will of their own.

Worrying hurts your head. Sort of like a Slurpee brain freeze, only different. But I couldn't stop.

What if they decided to turn *Real News* into their own little advertising leaflet? What if they marched into our offices and told Megan to write an editorial about how great their soda tasted?

Or told Ringo to draw his cartoon character, Simon, with a refreshing can of Crush? Or made me write a personality profile on the company president?

I'd be turned from a hard-hitting journalist into an advertising copywriter. Instantly.

And *Real News* would be turned into a *real snooze*.

Wishy-washy Editor
Sinks Paper!

I WOKE UP in a mood that would make a crabby bus driver seem like your favorite aunt.

I'm not a morning person to begin with, but after worrying myself to sleep with all the terrible stuff Crush might do to Trumbull, I woke up feeling like I'd been hit by a big truck. A big Crush Cola truck.

And I'd had a nightmare.

You know how sometimes when you dream you think you're really awake but you're just dreaming that you're awake? Well, in my nightmare, I turned off my alarm, got dressed and walked downstairs for breakfast. But when I walked into the kitchen, Gram was drinking Crush Cola. She pushed me out the door, and a Crush van drove me to school.

At school, big bottles of Crush lined the hallways. Kids roamed like zombies, hoisting Crush cans to their lips. And I couldn't get anyone to talk to me. They just kept mumbling, "Crush, Crush, I'm cool with the Crush." I ran from kid to kid, trying to get someone to say something else. I even pinged the cloned Kelleher twins on their shoulders, but it was as if I was snapping at air.

Then I saw Ringo walking away from me. I ran after him, but the hall kept getting longer. My legs felt like I was running in five feet of water. Carbonated water.

I finally got to Ringo. I grabbed his backpack and yanked him around. But, his . . . his eyes! Instead of the usual dark Ringo baby browns that see the world in their own killer way, they were little Crush bottle caps!

"Crush, Crush, I'm cool with Crush," he chanted. "Crush, Crush, I'm cool with Crush . . ."

I woke up to find my quilt tangled around my legs. But I was safe. At least the room wasn't filled with five feet of Crush Cola. I turned on the computer and logged on to e-mail the one person who always made my nightmares go away.

To: Doctormom
From: Wordpainter
   In great need of mother-daughter moment. Bad dream. No sleep. If you were

here, I'd fake a stomachache and claim bleeding out my eyeballs to stay home from that hive of a school. Please be momish and tell me I'm just going through a phase or something.

I hit Send and looked at the clock. It was early. Way early. But I was too spooked to go back to sleep. I decided to get some work done to take my mind off Crush Cola. Which was a good idea since I hadn't even looked at my Spanish book in two days. Plus the science lab story needed some attention.

I actually got a lot done, but by the time I dragged myself into the *Real News* office for our morning meeting, I was practically a zombie myself.

"Um, Casey, do you want to borrow my brush?" Megan asked.

"I'm fine," I muttered. I couldn't remember brushing my hair before I left the house, but after last night, the last person I wanted to talk to was Megan. Who, by the way, was dressed in head-to-toe lavender with blue-and-pink fake fur trim on her sleeves and collar. She also had fake furry hair clips, and glitter on her lips. She looked like a psychedelic elf.

I dropped my bag on Dalmatian Station and

plopped in a chair like I weighed about four hundred pounds. Dalmatian Station is our lime-green-and-black polka-dot table in the *Real News* office. I used to hate it, but it's kind of grown on me. It's where we all gather and put together the paper. A paper that used to take a stand on issues. Until today, when Megan would probably announce that Crush Cola was sponsoring a fashion feature on how you should match your soda flavor with your outfit.

I really did feel sick.

Ringo and Gary and Toni cruised in and grabbed seats.

"People, I have something to say before we start," Megan announced in a voice that was a little too loud.

I scowled and looked around. Ringo was staring at my hair.

"What?" I mouthed at him, but Megan was in full meeting mode.

"As you might have heard, Crush Cola wants to give the school money," Megan continued. "But they want something in return. Their logo on school property, and the right to sell their soda—only their soda—at Trumbull."

"Tyrants," I muttered.

"As you could probably guess," Megan added, "Casey has an opposing viewpoint. She feels that the students should have been asked before Trumbull agreed to this deal. And while at first I thought Casey was totally wrong . . ."

My ears perked up.

". . . I now think she has a point."

Suddenly I didn't feel so stepped on. Maybe there was hope. Maybe I wasn't the only sane person in the school. Maybe—

"I still disagree with Casey," she said, fiddling with the tiny pink bead on her tiny hoop earring.

Disagreement I could handle. It was lack of discussion that drove me nuts.

"I still think the sponsorship would help the school," Megan added. "But I also think the issue should be discussed by the student body. And in *Real News*."

I pinched myself. Maybe I was dreaming again.

"Man, Casey, you've got to wake up and smell the endorsements," Gary said, leaning back and plopping his high-tech sneakers on top of the table.

"Right now all I smell is a sour deal, made behind our backs," I said quickly.

"But endorsements are the name of the game," Gary said. "Look at Mia Hamm. Take Shaq O'Neill, or Tiger Woods. Do you think they made sour deals?"

Gary's a double threat: a jock and a brain. Put

the two together, and you get a know-it-all that can slam-dunk any argument. I like Gary, but I'll never understand how a person can spend all that time getting worked up over pointless point spreads.

"Endorsements are one thing, Gary. Buying the school off in every area is another," I said, wiping a crust from my left eye. I definitely didn't expect our resident sportswriter to side with me on this. And I hadn't even started investigating these Crush bullies, so I didn't have much ammo to argue with.

"Wrong again! Take a look at any sports team," he pointed out. "Not just the professional teams. Even Little League. Companies have money, and they want to use it to help out. It's only fair to give them a little something in return."

Gary was born with a silver football in his mouth, so I didn't really expect him to see the dark side of sponsorship.

Toni jumped in. "I don't know what the big deal is," she said as she tied her thick, orange-streaked curls into a knot on the top of her head. "Advertising is everywhere. There's a logo on everything, girl. Why get your freckles in a bunch over a company that wants to actually *pay money* to push their goods? Usually they just tell students, 'Here, this is cool. Buy this.'" She paused, then added, "And what's with your hair today? Did someone noogie you?"

I snorted at her. Did I warn you that Toni has attitude to burn? Secretly, I wish I had her iron fist. I mean, I'm stubborn, and I speak my mind when I have to, but she does it with a style that says, "Sit down, take notes."

"Advertising is everywhere," Toni went on. "You turn on the TV, there it is. You log on the Internet, bam! Another ad. Radio, magazines, who cares? Why not in school? You're going to buy this garbage or you're not. If you're brain-washed enough to do it because some ad tells you to, then you deserve whatever you get."

I narrowed my gaze at Toni, ready to deliver my speech that you couldn't let Crush crush us simply because ads were everywhere, when—

"Crush Cola!" Ringo piped up. "Ah, the sugary sweetness. The hiss of the opening bottle. The tingly feeling of bubbles going down my throat."

Et tu, Ringo? I couldn't believe he had just betrayed me like that.

"They have the greatest names for their flavors," Ringo said. "Grape isn't grape, it's 'Purple Explosion.' And cherry isn't just cherry, it's 'So Cherry It's Scary!' My tongue was red for three days last time I drank the stuff."

"And if the sports teams get uniforms, the

cheerleaders will get new uniforms, too," Gary added, egging Ringo on.

"Then again, I do believe in freedom of choice," Ringo said. "And that includes beverage choice. Because some people are really into chocolate milk. Which would be pretty good right about now."

"That's more like it," I sighed. "At least some-one—"

"But on the other hand," he said, looking from his right hand to his left, "if the money can help people, what does it matter what we're drinking? We can always bring milk from home. Perhaps that's just the price we pay." He looked thought-ful. "I don't know where I sit."

"You mean, where you stand?" Megan asked.

"No. Where I sit. In math class," he answered. "We moved our desks yesterday, and I don't re-member where mine is."

I had the urge to flick his ear. I couldn't claim Ringo as a total traitor, but he wasn't exactly siding with me either.

"I hate to interrupt this meeting of the minds," Mr. Baxter said, blowing into the office. He was late as usual, holding a huge stack of papers and a briefcase and a cup of coffee at the same time.

Besides being my English teacher, Mr. Baxter is the *Real News* advisor. He's a beefy man who always seems to be late for something, but he tries to be fair. When we were pulling the first newspaper together, he lent a hand without trying to leave his handprint everywhere.

"We have to decide exactly how *Real News* is going to approach this Crush issue," Mr. Baxter went on. "It's a hot topic—no doubt about it. Have you discussed how you want to present it?"

Finally. Some leadership.

"I say we split the editorial page," Megan said. "On one side, we have the pro argument. Gary can write that. He's got a great angle with the sports teams. And the con side would be Casey's. She's got . . . well, she's got her opinions."

"That works for me," I said, ignoring the dig.

"We need both pieces by this afternoon," Megan added. "We have to go to press tonight."

Gary groaned, but I knew I could write my piece during my free period. It was all in my head. I could already see the words coming together in my lead paragraph. My fingers itched to get going.

I started to get up as the first bell rang.

"There's one more thing," Megan said. "Casey, I think we should hold off on your science lab article until next week."

"Excuse me?" I spluttered. I had finished it in the wee hours of the morning and just needed to read it one more time before giving it to Megan.

"There's a chance it'll be old news before the issue comes out," she said. "The Crush arrangement might take care of the problem, so who's going to care? Instead, I'd like to run Gary's sports profile on the front page."

Mr. Baxter okayed the plan and rushed off like he suddenly remembered he had to meet someone.

I glared at Megan, who was busy rearranging her books in size order so she could carry them more efficiently. She knew as well as I did what canceling the story meant: I'd only have two dinky stories in the next issue—my SGA coverage and an editorial. Sure, the editorial was hot, but it wasn't front page. And it wasn't even a story. What kind of wishy-washy paper runs both viewpoints without reporting the story first? As the school paper, it was up to us to take a stand.

I grabbed my stuff and got ready to go. What else could I do? I'm not the editor in chief. Megan is. I could kick myself every time I think of how I voted for her instead of myself. Now *that* was an insane moment.

In math I kept thinking about how Gary's pointless profile was going to have the front page. My spot.

I couldn't get over the feeling that I was somehow letting the school down. People were used to seeing my byline, and knew I was hitting them with some serious information. They trusted me. I was their inside eyes. Now, all they were going to get was a puff piece on some athlete's foot.

"Casey? Are you with us?" Mr. Lanigan called from his desk. Caught zoning out by the Terminator. "I'd like to be so bold as to ask you to join the class and answer question ten."

He had been going down the rows with yesterday's homework assignment. Which I hadn't done because I was working on Spanish homework, and then on the science story, which Megan had just killed. I glanced at question ten. Luckily the kid who had my book last year had written in the answers on that page.

"I got square root nine," I answered, a little shaky.

"Very good, Casey. And that question was particularly difficult."

Termination avoided!

"Can you tell me what you did in step three of that problem to arrive at your correct answer?" he asked.

Maybe I had spoken too soon. I was tired, and math was not my favorite subject. I have a head for words. Not numbers.

"I could tell you, but then I'd have to kill you," I said.

The class snickered. Lanigan turned to put the problem on the blackboard, which meant I would have to go up and show my work.

"Psst, Casey!" I looked to my right and saw Keely Kelleher, one half of the Kelleher twins. "I'll give you my paper to copy up there, but you'll owe me one," she whispered quickly, stopping for a half second to stare at my head. "How 'bout it?"

Was the whole world one big back-scratching party? Does every little thing every person does have to get something in return?

"That's cheating, Keely. Get real."

"Well, fine," she said down her nose. "Don't say I didn't try to help."

Tried to blackmail, more like.

Just as I thought, This is it, my grades are going in the toilet with my writing career, Lanigan started doing the problem on the board.

"This is a very complex problem, so I'd rather work it out and explain what's happening," he said. "I assume that's fine with you, Casey?"

Fine? Try amazingly stupendous! Try fantabulously cool! For once this week I didn't feel like the girl with a big KICK ME sign on her back. I looked at Keely and flashed my toothiest grin, then licked my pinkie and wiped my eyebrow with it.

But Keely's little proposal got my wheels turning. Does everything have a price? And just because the school was getting money out of the deal, did that make it right? Was it even legal?

I needed some facts to back my opinion up.

While Gary was arranging his jock thoughts on the Crush issue, I was going to search the Net. I needed some core reasons why Trumbull shouldn't just roll over and drink their Crush like a good brainless doggie. I was going to write the kind of editorial that would get everyone talking. The first sentence would grab the reader by the neck. The rest of the piece would shake them sensible. And by the time everyone finished reading Casey Smith's editorial, they would be ready to march on the school lawn and protest this capitalist outrage.

MIDDLE SCHOOL STOMPS CRUSH TO SMITHEREENS!

I imagined news cameras arriving at Trumbull documenting the school that said no to corporate America. Your Constitution at work, ladies and gents. Step right up and express your point of view! Opinions NOT for sale!

I was feeling better. Maybe this was more than an editorial. Maybe there was a real, full story here.

Somehow, I had to find out what had happened in other schools that were offered commercial money. If I dug deep enough, I was bound to find something. This *had* to be news.

Suddenly, I knew exactly what to do.

Have fear, Crush Cola. Casey Smith, girl reporter, is here.

Rooster Girl Finds Dinosaur Eggs Hatching in Hair!

I WALKED OUT of math feeling ready to charge full speed ahead. Which I did, right smack into Tyler McKenzie.

"Hey! Watch it!" Tyler was holding his nose and looking at me like I just kicked a small pet. "Ah, man. This really hurts."

"Jeez . . . Tyler, I'm . . . sorry. I didn't . . . see you there. Coming down the hall, I mean. These hallways are dangerous. Especially after they mop. Slippery stuff. That floor polish stuff. Slip. Slide. Are you . . . are you okay?"

Who was this girl using my mouth to embarrass me?

"I'll live, I guess," he said, checking his hand to make sure there wasn't any blood. There was.

"Oh, just great. Do you have a tissue?" he asked tilting his head back.

"I think I have a napkin or something," I said, feeling a little panicked because I had just given Tyler a full-out nosebleed. I was digging around my bomb of a backpack when I felt a T-shirt. "Here's something," I said. But I couldn't get it out. So I yanked on it really hard until I managed to get it free. Just in time for it to whip up and snap Tyler's left ear.

"Aaahowweee!" he yelped. Physics was not my friend today. "What are you trying to do to me?" Now he was holding his nose *and* his ear. He looked like he was doing an impersonation of a telephone operator.

"Oh my gosh! Sorry! Here, here! Take this T-shirt. I got it free from Abbington Pools. It's old. I don't need it. I forgot it was there. I don't even go to those water slides anymore. Do you? Go to the water slides, I mean?"

I sort of shoved my T-shirt at him. And I guess I sort of don't know my own strength. Meaning: I sort of pushed him back a couple of steps, smack into a locker.

"Don't come any closer." Tyler rubbed the back of his head and held out his other hand to keep me at a distance.

I looked to my left and my right like a scared puppy. Had any of the kids spilling out of class noticed that I just beaten up Tyler MacKenzie?

"I'm . . . I'm really sorry," I said. "I was in a hurry because I have to write a story and I wasn't looking and . . . are you sure you're all right?"

He looked up me. He peered at my hair. Then he shook his head slowly, as if expecting to hear marbles rolling around. "Well I didn't expect to get hit by Hurricane Casey. But I guess my nose isn't broken." He balled up the bloody T-shirt and shot it into a trash basket in the hall.

"A point!" I said, trying to lighten the mood.

"That would be two points, but that's okay," he corrected me.

I felt stupid. Again.

"Um, I'm really sorry. I really am. Really." Do you think he really heard me?

"It's fine. I just have to get to second period," he said, adjusting his pack on his shoulders.

Then he turned and went around the corner faster than you can whip someone in the head with a T-shirt.

I went into the girls' bathroom to splash water on my face. I thought that would give me a clear head. When I looked in the mirror, it gave me something all right: a shot of humiliation. I had

60

about the goofiest hair I had ever seen in my life. I looked like I slept on glue. Or like the wind had frosted one side of my head. Hello, I'm Casey, Crazy Rooster Girl.

Did I mention I was mortified?

No wonder everyone had been staring at my hair all morning. And I talked to Tyler looking like this?

I finger-combed my brown mop as best I could. Then I pulled my baseball cap out of my pack and plunked it on. Just as I was finishing, Toni Velez strolled in.

"Casey, are you primping, girl?" she asked with an incredulous look on her face.

"My hair has a life of its own today," I said, suddenly self-conscious. "But I was just leaving."

She put her hands on her hips and smacked her chewing gum. "Uh-huh," she muttered with a grin on her face.

What did that mean?

I left the bathroom and started running down the hall when the tardy bell rang.

I was late for class. Again.

At least my next class was gym. I had seven more minutes to get into gear and into the gym. I can't stand gym class, but today was even worse since I didn't get much sleep. It seemed like I played volleyball for a million minutes before the bell sounded.

Finally. My free period. Time to get busy.

I went straight to the library and started researching on the Internet. I typed "school" and "sponsorship" in the title box of an on-line archive of old newspapers and magazine articles I had found. Jackpot! I had stories downloaded and printing faster than you can say "Rooster Girl" ten times.

I looked them over and found some pretty alarming stuff. Like one school in the Midwest that had televisions offered to them so the students could watch Congress. Which sounds good. But the company that wanted to sponsor them claimed to be an educational TV network. The network would only donate the TVs if their channel was the only one aired. Commercials included.

I was ready to march on Washington and protest right away! But I needed to get to the *Real News* office and start writing first. At least now I had some serious ammo to write a seriously scathing editorial.

I was practically running through the halls, clutching the bunch of printouts to my chest, when I spotted the tall, blond grinning puppet of the administration, Spencer. Interview time.

I stepped in his path.

"Oops, excuse me," he said, ever the politician. He looked down at me since he's really tall and I'm really not. Realizing he knew me from somewhere, he flashed me his winning (phony) smile.

"Have we met?" he asked.

"Sort of," I answered. "I'm Casey Smith, from the SGA meeting yesterday."

"Oh . . . yeah." The smile faded just a bit. It looked instead like he was baring his teeth.

"I've got to tell you," I said, standing up as straight as I could. "I'm writing an editorial for *Real News*, and I'm taking a position against the Crush sponsorship."

"Uh-huh?" His smile was quickly turning into a grimace.

"Yeah. I think the SGA should be taking a closer look at this contract Crush is offering Trumbull," I said. "I mean, you're supposed to represent the students, but I don't think you've given us a second thought."

"Look, Casey, I understand that you're concerned. But I don't see how there could be any problem with the sponsorship." He sounded condescending. Just like an eighth-grader.

"Oh no?" I held up the printouts and riffled through them. "Look at these. I've been doing some research, and you wouldn't believe how low some administrators have stooped to get corporate sponsorship. In New Jersey, there's a town where the students ride to school in buses shaped like giant weenies. Would that qualify as a problem in your book?"

Spence held up his hands as if I were coming at him with a whip and a chair. "Hey, look, I don't see that happening here," he said. "If you want to look into this, it's a free country. You can write whatever you want in your editorial. But be careful who you attack."

"What are you talking about?" I asked. "Is that a threat?" What was he going to do, have me doused with Crush?

"I'm not threatening. I'm just warning you," he said, gripping the straps of his backpack tighter. "Ms. Nachman has been working on this deal for months. She really wanted to land this contract, and she did. The Crush sponsorship is her baby. I don't think she'll appreciate opposition."

"Ms. Nachman?" I scowled.

"Yeah, Ms. Nachman," Spencer said. "If you make her look bad in front of the school board, it could give her a lot of trouble. There's more at stake here than a lousy logo on the football field. I don't think you know who you're fighting here. There are bigger forces at work."

"Uh, okay, Darth Vader," I scoffed. "I'll be sure

not to mess with the Death Star."

Spencer shook his head. "I'm serious," he said. "Before you go rushing in to attack everything, you might want to check out who you'd really be hurting."

"Get real," I told him. "While you're busy being cautious and careful and looking both ways for rich men in suits, I've got a job to do. And student interests to protect."

"Do what you think you have to do" was all he said before he walked away.

I watched him stalk down the hall, then I stomped off in the other direction. Wow, I could never run for public office. Those guys are always worrying about who they are going to offend.

But I guess it was a small victory he didn't stare at my hair.

I was only halfway down the hall when an arm reached out and yanked me into the girls' bathroom.

"Hey!" I yelled. I was suddenly face-to-face with a frantic Megan. She looked like an angry elf who had lost her powder puff.

"I saw you talking to Spencer," she said. "What were you saying?"

"I was warning him that I'm writing an editorial that's not going to make him happy," I said. "What's your problem?"

"Come on, Casey," Megan said. Her voice rose to a squealing pitch. "What were you saying?"

"Megan, what do you think? I was telling him about this research I was doing, stuff about other schools that have taken money from corporations." I held up my pile of papers like a shield. That seemed to slow Megan down a bit. She glared at the papers. "Are you sure that's all you were talking to him about?"

"Yeah, Megan, jeez," I said. "What else would I have to talk to that politician about?"

"Well . . . me," she said, backing down and leaning against a sink. "Maybe he thought it was my idea for you to take a position against Crush. I *am* the editor in chief of the paper."

And I don't know this? Newsflash.

"Listen, Megan, he knows it was my idea. I mean, he . . ." I stopped. Something was itching the inside of my brain. Megan was usually so level-headed and reasonable. She and I disagreed a lot, but she usually didn't lose her temper. And she never worried that my stories would reflect badly on her. When it came down to it, we both wanted *Real News* to be great.

There was only one reason for her to get her fake fur in a tangle over Spencer. She must like him!

I decided to have fun with this.

"Oh, wait," I said, pointing at her. "Come to think of it, there was some mention of you—"

"WHAT? He asked about ME? What did he say? How did he say it? Tell me! NOW!" She practically choked on her own spit.

I was right. She did like him. "Yeah, he did. He was telling me that he has a thing for girls who dress in really colorful getups."

"Oh my gosh! And I wore purple. It's perfect!" Her eyes were bulging out of her head. She was certifiably crazy.

"Gee, do you like Spencer, Megan?" I asked as innocently as I could.

"Like?" she asked, the same way you might say "Smallpox?"

Then she made a funny little "Nuh-uh" noise, and wiggled her head as if she'd just tasted something weird. She also blushed a hot pink that actually matched the fake fur on her collar. The girl matched even when she didn't try to match.

Then it hit me. I suddenly realized why Megan was so pro-Crush. She was pro-Spencer. I could tease her about liking Spencer, but not about letting it interfere with her opinions.

"I can't believe this," I grumbled. "No wonder you won't take a position on the Crush sponsorship. You're rolling over and playing dead because you want this guy Spencer to like you!"

"That is so ridiculous," she spat.

"What kind of journalist are you?" I went on. "What do you think would happen if the editor in chief of *Newsweek* killed an important story because he had the hots for a member of city council?"

"The hots?" Megan's jaw clenched. "I have no hots. I don't get hots. And if I did, I wouldn't let the hots cloud my judgment."

"Oh, right!" I slapped the sink. "You're just selling out the student body. Keeping this thing off the front page. Diluting my editorial with an opposing viewpoint. No, your judgment's not clouded at all! You're hots-impaired, if you ask me."

"Casey!"

"Don't 'Casey' me!" I snapped. "Where is your integrity? Your journalist's objectivity?"

"There is nothing wrong with looking at both sides of an issue," she shot back, folding her arms on her chest dramatically. "My decision to run both viewpoints instead of a front-page story has nothing to do with my feelings for Spencer. And I hate to break it to you, but you just don't have front-page material!"

"Don't count on that, Hots Girl," I said, stacking my printouts and slipping them into a folder. "I've got more than you think here."

"Well, I'm not sure you do," Megan said. "And don't go blaming me if whatever you're trying to dig up doesn't turn out to be a real story."

She stalked out of the bathroom. I turned to follow her, but paused in the doorway.

That's when I decided to let her go. I wanted to keep arguing, but there was no reasoning with her.

She was way too crushed on Spencer.

Megan O'Connor had it bad.

Virus Reaches Epidemic Proportions—No Vaccine in Sight!

THAT MADE TWO huge arguments in one day. My head was throbbing. My stomach was rumbling. I needed some chocolate.

And a dose of refreshing Ringo perspective.

After school, I trudged over to the Friday afternoon cheerleading practice to find Ringo. The guy is a little left of center, but at least he stands out from the crowd. And right now, I felt like the whole crowd was suffering from a severe case of lovesickness. Megan loved Spencer. Ms. Nachman loved Crush Cola. And I hated all of it.

I sat down on a bleacher and dug around in my pack. I found a half-full bag of chocolate-covered peanuts and started munching while I watched Ringo do his thing.

I had to admit, Ringo was really doing okay as

a cheerleader. He was fearless, doing all those back flips and cartwheels and handsprings. And he was stronger than I thought, letting girls stand on his shoulders and stooping over at the bottom of a big, giggling pyramid.

Letting cheerleaders walk all over you wasn't my idea of fun, but then again, writing stories wasn't his.

He loped over to me during a break in the action and perched on top of the metal fence.

"C-A-S-E-Y!" he cheered. "Our resident anti-Crush activist. How's the fight going for refreshing, carbonated justice?"

"Ugh, Ringo, it's insane," I groused, shielding my eyes from the sun. "I mean, it's one thing to go up against Ms. Nachman and Spencer Woodham. Now it turns out I have to do battle with Megan, too."

"Battle," Ringo said thoughtfully. "Yes, the two of you are like warriors sometimes. Long-haired, sneaker-wearing warriors. But you can sink her battleship."

"Well, yeah," I said, holding out some peanuts to Ringo. "The thing is, Megan has a crush on that Spence guy. I bet she thinks if she kisses up to him, he'll ask her to the dance. Only she's in sixth grade and he's in eighth. So how likely is that? It's so complicated. I feel like I could fall off this bleacher just thinking about it."

"Well, if it helps, I'm totally on your side of the fence," Ringo said. Looking down at the metal fence between field and bleachers, he added, "Even though I'm on the other side of the fence right now."

"You are? What changed your mind?"

"I thought about it and decided to be on your side. Metaphorically. Not literally."

"Thanks for pointing that out," I said. "It's all much clearer now."

"Hey, Ringo!" One of the cheerleaders came bounding over. I don't know what those girls' bones are made of, but it must be some kind of rubber. "This is Casey, right?"

"No, it's Casey *Smith*," he said.

She giggled as if he'd just made the greatest joke in the world. That made him smile, and his chest puffed out a little. I didn't think he was making a joke. I mean, that's just how he talks. But the cheerleader acted like he was the most hysterical comedian she ever heard.

"I'm Samantha," she said to me. "Samantha Rodelle. Ringo told me you're going up against the Crush Cola plan. That's awesome."

"Really?" That was nice of her.

"Totally!" Her face got serious. "I can't have too much sugar. I'm hypoglycemic. Plus it's so fattening! I like to drink Diet Cool, and if I can't get it at school, I'm going to be really bummed."

"Hypoglycemic," Ringo repeated, like it was a piece of poetry. "Hype. Oh. Gloss. See Mick—"

"Nice to meet you, Casey," Samantha interrupted Ringo's musings. "Ringo, we gotta keep practicing!" She bounced back to practice. I glared at Ringo.

"Diet Cool," he said, watching Samantha bob down the field. "Tasty."

"Oh, Ringo," I moaned. Not Ringo too. The crush had gotten him.

"Not only am I totally grossed out," I said. "I also suspect that Samantha and her Diet Cool habit are the real reasons why you're suddenly so gung-ho against Crush."

Ringo tilted his head and made funny, rubbery faces at me. "My aunt Gracie used to have a cat named Samantha," he said. "It liked to hide in the neighbor's garage."

I ignored his diversion. "Don't get me wrong. I need all the support I can get." I backed away from the fence. "But I just wish someone would think about this with a clear head. Not a love-filled one." I had to go write. I couldn't stand around and watch Ringo flirt with Samantha for another second.

"Casey, there's room in my head for lots of

things," he called after me as I walked away. "For instance, did you know that about thirteen million pieces of candy corn are eaten every Halloween?"

"What does that have to do with anything?" I asked over my shoulder.

"Nothing!" Ringo stood up and balanced on top of the fence, his arms outstretched. "C-A-S-E-Y!"

"Ringo, whatever your head is filled with, we should bottle that," I said, and flashed him a grin so he would know I wasn't mad. Even though he'd joined the Love-Struck Zombie Club.

Dance Flu was one powerful virus.

I hurried back to the *Real News* office and started typing furiously. It took about two hours to whip my editorial into almost-done status.

Which is what I did. Brilliantly, if I do say so myself.

The main points of the story were that the SGA president, Spencer Woodham, had confirmed that Principal Nachman had been working on this deal for months. It was a cloak-and-dagger, behind-the-scenes scheme.

Rereading my page, I got steamed all over again. We were lied to with silence. We were lied to every time we had an SGA meeting, and Principal Nachman didn't show up to tell us she was working on this plan. And we weren't the only ones. The school board was fed a bunch of silent lies, too.

I sharpened it up with a few spicy examples of how sponsorship had changed other schools. The story of the school buses painted with giant hot dogs was one of my favorites. Weenie buses. Unbelievable.

Then I told the students to ask themselves some hard questions. Don't the students have a say in the contracts our school signs? Don't adults keep telling us that life is all about making the right choices? Shouldn't we be allowed to make this choice ourselves?

I ended it by demanding that the students not allow these lies to go on. Step up! I wrote. Let your voice be heard! Don't get sold to the Crush Corporation. Fight the power!

I hit Print and stared at my fingernails. I waited by the printer like an expectant father. And when my page slid out, I held it up with both hands and looked at it like it was my new baby.

Then I couldn't help myself—I kissed the paper!

This editorial masterpiece was going to rock the boat at Trumbull.

Big-time.

Editorial Wakes Up
Hibernating Students

"HIGH FIVE, CASEY!" Two voices chimed together.
I turned around and saw the Kelleher twins,
Kendall and Keely. Both girls grinned identically.
Both held up their perfectly matched right
hands.

"I think this would qualify as a high ten," I
said, giving them each a satisfying smack.

Monday.

I was barely through the front doors of school,
but I could smell the controversy in the air. A
quick glance at the empty *Real News* baskets told
me that I had been right: The Crush issue was
hot. Every newspaper had been snatched up!
Students were probably debating my editorial
over hash browns in the cafeteria right now. And
judging from the Kelleher clones, I might even

76

have a chance at getting people on my side.

"Thanks a lot, Smith," said a gruff voice behind me.

I turned and found myself staring at the chest of one of Gary's friends from the football team. Was that steam coming out his ears? Or did reading make his brain smoke?

"Was it something I wrote?" I asked innocently, hoping he wouldn't stick a football up my nose.

"Leave it to someone who's never played a sport in her life to ruin it for the rest of us," he growled. "Tell you what. You play a game in a five-year-old helmet that's too small, and tell me how you like it. Then you can complain about all the money spent on our equipment. Stupid girl."

Except for the last comment, I couldn't really let that guy get under my skin. He had his brains in his biceps. I had a mission.

I walked a victory walk down the halls. I could tell that some people were peeved at me and some were digging my story. Either way, I won. Why? Because they all had an opinion. Maybe my story wasn't a hundred percent popular. Maybe I hadn't won the whole school to my side. But I made people think.

That felt really awesome.

I strutted into the *Real News* office. Gary was lounging with his feet up. Toni was sitting on a desk in her oversized overalls and tank top, kicking her legs against a chair.

"Girl, everybody's talking about you," she said.

"No kidding," Gary grumbled. "Man, you really get excited. I just wrote my opinion. You wrote this serious piece with facts and stats and stuff."

I ignored him.

"Toni, what did *you* think of my editorial?" I asked. "I mean, do you still think it's not worth dealing with? Did I come on too strong?" I really wanted to ask if she loved it, but that would have been major compliment-fishing.

She shrugged. "I just heard a lot of people talking about it," she said, fiddling with a camera.

"But what about the part where I talked about advertising, and how it's everywhere? I got that from you, and then I made the point that—"

"Casey, I don't remember," Toni said grumpily. She stood up and walked over to her photo file and started digging around. "You expect me to memorize your whole editorial? When's this meeting going to start, anyway? I gotta go."

"Hang on," Mr. Baxter said, entering the office with Megan and Ringo behind him. "Sit back down, Toni. I just have a few things I want to say."

The meeting was in progress.

"I want to get right to the point," Mr. Baxter

said. "Gary, nice work. You made your points concisely, and you rounded out your argument well."

I sat there, a little flustered from Toni's brush-off, but waiting eagerly for Baxter to turn that heap of praise on me.

"Casey . . ." he stopped. "I think you . . . well, this was supposed to be an editorial. There's a difference between reporting and suggesting that people should riot."

That wasn't exactly the praise I was expecting to hear.

"I wanted to stir things up," I told him. "I wanted to get people talking."

"I understand that, Casey," Mr. Baxter said. "That's a good editorial position, but you don't want to stir things up with a stick of dynamite."

"Yeah, dynamite would blow," Ringo chimed in. Megan shot him a "Now is not the time" look.

"Mr. Baxter, I can handle this," I said firmly.

He exhaled loudly, then looked at his watch. That was usually his cue to scurry off in a hurry. Which was a relief because I believed in my mission and I didn't want anything to spoil this day. I just wasn't in a mood to argue. And for me, that's a pretty darn good mood.

I grabbed my bag, tossed off a general good-bye to the room and left to get to class on time. For a change. But it was slow going. Every couple of feet I had to stop and debate with someone the pros and cons of the Crush contract. Or accept a high five. Or return a scowl.

I was sort of a celebrity.

I was also sort of annoyed. I was there to make the students think. Not make them think out loud at *me*. Couldn't they talk to each other? I wondered if I would be needing a wig and some dark glasses. I really didn't want all this attention.

That is, until Tyler came up to me.

I was discussing the low nutritional value of Crush with that vegetarian girl from the SGA meeting when I felt a tap on my shoulder. Having been tapped, yelled at, called over and challenged about my editorial for the last fifteen minutes nonstop, I didn't even look over my shoulder.

"In a second!" I said with the patience of a caffeinated teacher.

I felt the tap again. Only this time it was harder, like a jab, right on my shoulder bone.

"Whoever you are, you're about to. . . ." As I spun around, I saw Tyler and completely lost my train of thought. "Uh, hey, that hurt," I finished, rubbing my shoulder.

"I owed you," he said, tapping his nose.

I looked at him with not a thought in my brain. Me, Casey Smith. Why do I get so gooney and dumb around Tyler?

"I think your story is killer," he said. "I just finished reading it in the cafeteria and I think you're right on the mark. Especially that stuff about how Ms. Nachman was lying to us by not telling the truth all along." He shifted his feet a little and added, "The way you put it? 'Lying with her silence.' Very cool."

Tyler McKenzie quoting my story? "Wow," I said. "Thanks." I felt a weird hot prickly feeling on the back of my neck. Was I breaking out in hives? I scratched my neck and looked at the ground.

"So, listen, I had this idea," he said. "I was in the admin office just now, and I heard Ms. Nachman saying the Crush people are going to be here on Wednesday and Thursday. They're planning some kind of pep rally for their soda, and they're going to hand out free caps and T-shirts, stuff like that. I guess they think we'll be all excited to get a free ugly hat."

"Yeah, right," I said, not feeling so hot and dumb all of a sudden.

"My big idea was that we could have some kind of protest," he said. "We could wear T-shirts or whatever from a rival soda company, maybe. Something like that. What do you think?"

My wheels spun. "A protest!" I repeated. Instantly I thought of what my gram had told me about how she'd seen local townspeople shut

down a dangerous nuclear power plant by protesting. Alone, she said, each of those people was
powerless. But together, they shut down an environmental nightmare.

"That sounds like a terrific idea," I said. "What
if we made a human chain and blocked the school
doors so the Crush people couldn't enter the
building? Or should we just wear the rival stuff
and make signs and be this anti-Crush menacing
presence?"

"Human chain, Casey?" Tyler said. "That
might be a little . . . much." He bit his lip, then
went on, "What if when the people from Crush get
here they find us all drinking Diet Cool? Or Zing.
Or even milk."

It wasn't as dramatic as a human chain, but
I could live with it. And I couldn't believe that
Tyler had thought this whole thing through.
Could it be his brain worked like mine?

"You rock, Tyler!" I said grabbing his arm. It
felt warm through the soft flannel of his shirt, and
I let go of it immediately. "I mean, your plan . . .
rocks. Good plan. Really."

"Thanks," he said. "I wouldn't have thought to
do all this if I hadn't read your story."

Whoo, it *was* hot in the hallway today.

I sucked in some air. "I'm just psyched that

I'm not the only one who hates the idea of Crush taking over the school," I said. "So, um, should we just tell people to bring in whatever rival products and stuff they can scrounge up?"

"Sure. But I've got another plan, too," he said, leaning in and lowering his voice. "I don't want to say it out loud yet because I have to check with someone. But I want to tell you about it. Give me your phone number and I'll call you tonight. Soon as I have it all straight."

"My phone number?" I repeated, as if he asked for a blood sample.

"Yeah." He grinned, and I noticed that he had one tooth that was a little bit crooked. Right in front. It made his smile sort of lopsided, in a nice way. "You know. The phone? It's this new invention where you talk into a device to communicate with another person."

"Right," I said, laughing way too loud. "I've heard of that." I pulled out my notebook and wrote my name and number on a piece of paper. I looked at my plain, nonbubbly, no-frills handwriting. Was I dreaming again? I handed him the paper.

He waved it at me as he walked away. "Fight the power," he said over his shoulder.

"Don't believe the hype," I answered, feeling like I had been crowned queen of the hallways.

I stuffed my notebook back into my pack, then stopped for a second and pictured what the protest would look like on Wednesday. Smiling, I zipped up my bag and floated down the hallway.

Then the second bell rang. Dang!

After school, I headed home to check the ringer on my phone. Functional. Then I went on-line. First I reread the e-mail that I'd gotten from my mother over Friday night.

To: Wordpainter
From: Doctormom
So sorry you had a nightmare. But I bet you've already figured out why, what, where and how to deal with it. Although I should ask you, did you eat anything right before you went to bed? Does it to me every time. Easy on the chocolate, Ms. Smith. Hang in there, kiddo. And have something green for dinner!

Geez, Casey, I wish I was there with you. I know that you and Gram are two peas in a pod, but I do miss you. Every day. We could use your sense of humor around here.

Promise me that you will most definitely

let me know if you need me. And remember, this isn't forever.

Write back soon.

Just reading over it one more time made me smile. Mom's e-mails always do. I e-mailed Mom the latest news. Then I sent an instant message to Griffin. He needed to know about my instant celebrity status.

To: Thebeast
From: Wordpainter
Mission accomplished . . . almost. Students are hot under the collar. Teachers miffed. Tyler found me in the hall and hatched a devilish plan to stage a protest! He's calling tonight. But don't you start with me. Strictly business.

To: Wordpainter
From: Thebeast
Rock on with your bad self, Casey Smith! You did it . . . almost. A protest sounds like the best thing. But how are you going to find out what's the real deal behind this deal? As for Tyler? I won't start, but I'll sing: Two little students sitting in a tree, p-r-o-t-e-s-t-i-n-g. . . .

Infuriating! I can't stand that kind of teasing. Or the subject of who-likes-who in general. I do *not* like Tyler McKenzie. Let me repeat. I do not like Tyler. At all. That way.

I wrote "Ha, ha" and hit Send. Then I logged off and started in on all the extra homework I had because of my new tardiness problem. Great. More homework. My favorite.

When I finished the last of the thirty math problems the Terminator had assigned, I lay down on my bed. I hugged a red silk Chinese pillow and stared out the window, thinking about how my editorial had rocked Trumbull. I couldn't help but smile to myself. This was real journalism. I was a real journalist.

Brrriinnnggg! I nearly jumped out of my skin.

"Casey, telephone," Gram said, poking her head in my room.

"I'll be right there," I said, hopping up and checking my hair in the mirror.

"It's a boy."

"Must be Griffin."

"Nope," she said. "Definitely not Griffin." She tapped her fingers on the doorway and smiled. I put my hand on the phone and just looked at her. She knew when to back off. Besides, Tyler was just calling to talk about our plan. It's not like he was calling about the stupid dance or anything.

I picked up the phone. "Hello?"

"Casey, I have great news!" Tyler's voice was different on the phone. Deeper. And a little scratchy. "I think I know someone who can help us out with the protest."

"Killer," I said. "Let's hear it."

"I found someone who'll donate fifty T-shirts with the logo for Zing Cola!"

"No you didn't!" I shouted.

"I did," he said. "I'm picking them up tomorrow after school. I can bring them in Wednesday morning."

"Tyler, you're amazing," I said. "Do you think they'll give us soda, too?"

"I'm not sure yet," he answered. "I would, if I were them. It's a chance to really irritate their rivals."

"And get kids hooked on their disgusting soda," I pointed out. "We're all going to be burping sugar fiends in Zing T-shirts."

Tyler laughed. "Casey, let's worry about one thing at a time," he said. "I just want to send Crush a message: They don't own our school!"

"You go, boy!" I said, suddenly thinking that that was the dumbest saying ever invented. I toned myself down. "Um, you're right. They don't own our school. We'll make them hear us."

"We're gonna to do more than that," he said. "We're going to take back our school."

"And," I finished, "we're going to crush Crush!"

Mystery Vandal Derails Protest!

I WOKE UP early on Tuesday feeling energized. I zoomed through the rest of my homework, came up with a couple of slogans for signs, e-mailed Griffin again and organized my sock drawer. I wished I could fast-forward through Tuesday and get straight to Wednesday. We were going to give Crush a run for its money.

While I ate cereal for breakfast, I looked in my notebook at the sign slogans I had come up with:

> Trumbull Can't Be Bought!
>
> Students Not for Sale!
>
> We Won't Be Crushed!
>
> Give Crush a Run for Its Money!

I picked up my cereal bowl and drank the sugary milk. Nothing like some Honey Bombs to start a growing girl's day off right. Then I kissed Gram on the cheek as she read the paper, grabbed my backpack and started for school.

As I passed manicured lawns and clapboard houses, I could hear Tyler's voice buzzing through my head. For some reason, I kept going over our phone conversation. I couldn't believe I really said "You go, boy!" I hear Toni say it all the time. But it definitely didn't work for me.

The more I tried to not think about that phone call, the more it popped into my head: *What was that about?*

As I neared school, I saw Tyler standing with a clump of people just by the front doors. The Kelleher twins were nearby. They looked at me, then turned and whispered frantically to each other.

"Casey!" Tyler called, and waved me over.

April, the juice girl from the SGA meeting, was standing with him. "Did you hear?" she asked.

"Hear what?" I looked at Tyler.

"Someone vandalized all the Crush vending machines," Tyler practically shouted. "They stuck slugs in the coin slots and now they're all jammed and have to be replaced. Every single one!"

"All of them?" My eyebrows shot up. "On purpose?"

"Definitely," Tyler said. Then he leaned in to me. "This was a message."

"A message?" I said. "I wanted people to take a stand, to do something, but—

"I know. I wish I'd thought of it myself!" Tyler beamed.

"No, no, you don't understand," I said holding up my hand. "It's wrong to vandalize property."

He shifted his notebooks from one hand to the other. I noticed that he was wearing kind of a cool, hipster shirt, sort of like a bowling shirt.

"Casey Smith to the principal's office." The booming voice over the loudspeaker interrupted my thoughts. "CASEY SMITH, PLEASE REPORT TO THE PRINCIPAL'S OFFICE AT ONCE!"

Uh-oh.

"What do you think it's for?" Tyler asked.

"Ohmigosh," April yelped. "I hope they don't think you did it!"

"There's no way," Tyler offered. "But they might—"

"Guys! Guys! Don't sweat it," I said, backing away from them. "I can handle it." I spun around and almost kissed the Kelleher twins in the process. "Excuse me, Kelleher squared." They just stared at me as I stepped around them.

Although I'd acted low-key with Tyler and April, my guts were twisted into knots as I plodded to the office. They couldn't pin this on me. Could they? I mean, I knew I didn't do it. But what if they didn't know I didn't do it? Did they know who did it? And anyway, who did do it?

I had a headache by the time I got to Ms. Nachman's office. I barely had time to sink into a chair before the principal lashed out.

"That is *it*!" Ms. Nachman was livid. She pounded on her desk with her fist and sent a pencil flying across the room. "Have you heard that our vending machines were vandalized?"

"Yeah, but I didn't—"

"Casey, I don't think you did it," she said, clearly trying to control her rage. "But it was your editorial that got the students whipped into a frenzy. You're creating extremely antisocial behavior. I want you to stop writing about Crush in the student paper. Immediately."

Stop writing? Clearly Ms. Nachman had lost her mind.

"You can't tell me what to write!" I shouted like a spoiled child. "That's censorship! That's un-American!"

Ms. Nachman made a frustrated noise and stared at me hard. "I run this school, Casey Smith. And I can't let you write editorials that cause damage to the school." She was so stern, so much like a politician in her suit and hair-sprayed hair.

"But this is *our* school, Ms. Nachman," I said, giving her my best hairy-eyeball stare. "I am not personally causing damage. I'm reporting the news. Your students are doing what they want with the information. Information they have a right to know. This stuff affects their lives."

"Think your position through, Casey," she said tightly. "Are you prepared to face your fellow students if we don't take the money, and as a result they don't have adequate science lab equipment? What about the auditorium? One of these days, that ugly falling plaster is going to become a hazard. Without funding, we'll have to shut the whole thing down. Would that help the students? Not having an auditorium?"

"There have to be other ways," I said. "I stand by my story. We should have a vote on whether to take the money. Let the majority decide. Then I'll put a cork in it."

"There's more," Ms. Nachman said, straightening her blouse.

I shifted in my seat. My headache was getting worse.

"When you write editorials that make people want to act, then you're partly responsible for their actions," she went on. "Whoever vandalized those vending machines didn't hurt anyone this time. But vandalism can escalate into something more serious."

"You can't blame the media for what one kid does," I said confidently. My many conversations with Gram had taught me that crucial bit of info.

"Well, not entirely." She crossed her arms. "But you do have an effect on people. That's a responsibility. A responsibility you need to take seriously."

Adults are always talking about responsibility this, responsibility that. Do they think kids don't get the concept? Do they think we only care about Saturday morning television?

"I have a responsibility to tell the truth," I said, looking right at her. "I take that very seriously."

When Ms. Nachman finally let me go, I stepped into the hall and breathed a sigh of relief. Another battle over. But I was still bugging out on the vandalized machines. I was glad that someone had taken action against Crush, but destroying stuff is going over the line.

And another thing: What if there was backlash? Against me? If Ms. Nachman blamed me for the vandalism, what was to stop other people from pointing a finger my way?

I realized that the best thing to do was find out who had vandalized the machines. If I could discover their identity, I could go to them and get them to join Tyler's legal, peaceful protest. That would stop the vandalizing, keep everyone out of trouble and get a strong supporter for our side.

I sat down against a locker and opened my notebook:

DATELINE: Tuesday, first period, post-Nachman tongue-lashing

CRUSH VANDALISM:

Crime was committed after school.

Most after-school activities are outside on the playing fields, in the gym, or in the pool.

Some are in classrooms, but mostly on the first floor.

CONCLUSION: The cafeteria was wide open.

Anyone who's not in a club could have sneaked in and done it.

The bell rang and the hallway erupted into a chorus of slamming lockers, footsteps and voices. The cafeteria was on my way to gym, so I decided to check in with Mrs. Stekol, my favorite cafeteria lady.

"Hey, Barbara Walters!" she called out from behind the trays of steaming food.

"Mrs. Stekol, I hear there was some trouble here last night," I said, eyeing the blobs of gravy she was ladling onto meat.

"Yes. Is very bad for school. And students," she said. "The brand-new machines—they ruined them!"

"It's too bad," I agreed. "I don't suppose you saw anyone?"

"Principal Nachman ask me already," she said, wiping her hands on her apron. "I was very, very busy last night. I make the meatballs for tomorrow's Surprise Lunch. But shh! Don't tell. It's a secret! You want to try some?"

She opened a large metal freezer door and showed me a tray full of boiled tennis balls.

"Uh." I stepped back. "That's quite a surprise there. And thank you so much, but I usually bring my lunch."

"Eh, your loss." She shrugged, closing the door.

Yeah, I did lose something: my appetite.

I thanked Mrs. Stekol and headed to gym. For once I was on time, but I had to take a minute to finish my entry in my notebook.

WITNESSES:

Mrs. Stekol: Too engrossed in surprise meatballs to notice anything.

NEXT MOVE: ???????

NOTE TO SELF: Remember Griffin's advice: Chill out. Wait for things to develop.

Editorial Staff Overcome by Toxic Dance Fumes!

LUNCHTIME. THE *Real News* office. Update meeting.

I plopped my bag down on Dalmatian Station and pulled out my lunch. I found a peanut butter and banana sandwich, a bag of chips, some carrots and a box of orange juice. My lunch was about as far from Meatball Surprise as it could get. Good ol' Gram.

"Congratulations, everyone!" Megan said. I noticed that her sandwich had the crust cut off, the white bread dissected into neat squares. And she had several cookies stacked neatly in front of her. Sugar cookies. Of course. "The editorials really struck a nerve," she said, lifting a dainty sandwich square.

Editorial*s*? I thought. Try editorial. As in one. *Mine.*

"I think we should go forward with the momentum," Megan continued. "My thoughts were that we should take a student poll on the Crush issue. I've written up a questionnaire and made copies for everyone. You should all grab a clipboard and try to get responses throughout the day. We can publish the results in the next *Real News*. And make sure you ask different people what they think—not just the people you agree with, Casey."

I rolled my eyes. "Like I'd really do that." First she doesn't give me credit for striking the big Trumbull nerve center. Then she accuses me of one-sided reporting. I wanted to flick her cookies out of their neat little stack.

"Ringo?" she continued. "Do you have any ideas for a Simon cartoon with this issue in it?"

"I'm on it, chief," he said, his mouth full of something. What, I don't know. Not that I wanted to. Ringo's lunches are . . . creative. "Check this out."

"This is your brain after Crush Cola."

We all leaned in to the center of Dalmatian Station and looked at Ringo's sketch.

Toni laughed. "Simon is totally bugged out."

"I don't know, Ringo," Megan said, biting her lip.

"Come on, Megan," I pleaded. "Unscrew your hair clip and loosen up. It's a great cartoon."

She touched the clip in her hair and frowned at me.

"Okay, fine. Run it," she said. I was impressed. For once orderly Megan didn't overthink something. "Casey, you know that research you were working on?" she asked, not looking at me as she spoke.

I held my breath. Was I finally getting a chance to slap this thing on the front page where it belonged?

"I want you go forward with that story," she said. "Write about corporate sponsorship in schools for the next issue's front page."

I almost spit out a banana chunk.

"Woo!" I yelped, throwing both hands in the air like I was in the front car of a roller coaster.

"Hold on a second," Gary said, scowling at Megan. "You're giving Casey freedom to trash this thing? You're going to kill the Crush deal!"

Megan shook her head, giving us her Madame Editor "I'm serious" look. "I'm counting on Casey for a wide perspective. Don't just tell stories of weenie buses. If there are schools where the corporate sponsorship worked well, please be honest about that."

"Got it," I said. Megan is the Princess of Priss, but she also has some pretty good editor instincts.

"I'm not sure you do," Gary said, waving a disk at me. "Did you forget that *Real News* is on the list to get funding from Crush Cola?"

"Of course not," I said. "But I won't be bought."

"It's not *you* I want to buy," Gary said, waving a floppy disk at me. "Do you know what that stupid Disktop software did to me? I had every team roster stored on here, and now the disk is ruined. I can't even read it on my own PC. Disktop ate all my data."

"How's that for indigestion?" Ringo added.

"Hey, I've lost stuff on Disktop, too," I said. "But there's got to be a better way to get the money for new equipment."

"We've always talked about bake sales. Or a car wash," Megan said.

Toni and I winced at each other.

If only we were in one of those schools with a wealthy graduate who'd donate money, no strings attached. There'd be a computer on every desk. Three swimming pools. Comfortable chairs in the media center.

I grabbed a clipboard to check out the survey. Walking up to strangers and asking them their opinions on stuff wasn't really my style. But I was driven by my new story. Besides, it would be a great way to sniff around for clues about who had vandalized the machines. I could talk to people I normally wouldn't have any reason to bug in the hallway.

My eyes skimmed the form. It was a little, well, fluffy. Cutesy fluffy. And leave it to Megan to print hearts around the border.

"So, Toni," Megan said, "what are you wearing to the dance?"

Oh, no. Not *that* again.

Toni looked up from her container of cold spaghetti and pointed a fork at Megan. "Girl, I scored the flyest gear at the mall this past week-end," she crowed. "I spent a month's baby-sitting money because I had to buy two different outfits. I couldn't decide which one I wanted. So I figure I can just return the one I decide not to wear."

"Or you could wear them both," Ringo said. "Halfway through the dance, you could change. Just to mess with people's heads."

"Yeah, I could do that—if I was a freakazoid," Toni said, pinging him on the shoulder. "I can't decide if I want to look really nice or really chill."

"Oh, Toni!" Megan shook her head. "You *have* to wear a dress! You look like a tomboy every day! Don't you want to look different?"

Oh, Megan! Oh, Toni! Who cares?

"Guys, we still have to talk about this poll a little more," I said, holding up the clipboard. No one even heard me.

The First Dance Flu. It had gone into overdrive and infected the whole staff.

"So I guess you're wearing a dress," Toni said.

"I have no idea what I'm wearing." Megan held her hands up and looked like she was contemplating the greatest decision of her life. "I looked in my closet, and I have nothing. Nothing!"

"Man, you girls," Gary moaned. "Nobody's going to notice what you're wearing."

"Oh, Mister Cool," Toni scoffed. "And I guess the girl you asked is wearing a clown costume?"

Gary shifted in his seat. Was he blushing?

"You do have a date, right?" Toni teased. "There must be some lucky girl. Like, oh I dunno, that girl from the swim team? Natalie?"

Gary laughed uneasily, like a sickly machine gun. "I'm going with a bunch of guys from the team. But I have it on good authority that the swimmer in question is also going with a group of girls."

"You have a dating authority?" Ringo piped up. "Is that like a phone hot line?"

"Nah." Gary tossed his baseball cap at Ringo. "Why, is there someone you're thinking of asking?"

"Sa-man-tha," Ringo said, pronouncing the name as if it was a prayer. "I don't know if she'll say yes. I'm thinking about asking Kelli Catrice if she'll find out if Samantha likes me. But if I could use your dating authority . . ."

Weren't we just having a newspaper meeting and talking about important stuff a minute ago?

"Why bother with Kelli?" I told Ringo. "Why not just leave an anonymous note on Samantha's locker asking her to list all the guys she'd like to go with?"

I meant that as a joke, but Ringo looked thoughtful.

"Do you think that list would work?" he asked.

"Would you all please find your brains and insert them back into your skulls!" I hollered. "We have work to do, people. I, for one, do not have time to get all dolled up for some dance where I'm going to stand around and scratch every itch my ugly-fugly dress gives me. I've got better things to do than drink pink punch and slow-dance with a goober from math class. Thanks, but no thanks."

My mouth was off and running again.

Toni giggled. "Girl, you need to chill."

"I do *not*! There's work to do, and all you guys do is sit around and talk about the dance and Samantha or Tyler or . . ."

I meant to say Spencer, not Tyler.

Megan shot Toni a look. Toni smacked her gum and grinned.

Great. Just great. The last thing I needed was Toni jumping on the tease-Casey-about-Tyler bandwagon. The truth was I really didn't adore the idea of getting all frilled up to stand around at this dance. But I guess I kind of, sort of, *maybe* thought that it could possibly by chance be fun. If Tyler went. But only because he understood my battle with Crush.

Not because I like him or anything.

"I'm going out and getting surveys answered and doing my job," I said without looking at anyone. I grabbed my backpack and a clipboard. "You guys can stay here and decide what to wear until dawn for all I care."

Twins Have Psychic Bond That Chokes!

AFTER I STORMED out of the meeting, I lost some of my steam. This dance thing was really getting to me. Time to regroup.

Out in our schoolyard there's a huge tree that creates a nice patch of shade. Finding a spot by the brick wall of the school, I sat down and hugged my legs. The wind moved the branches, and sunlight bounced off the shiny leaves. It almost looked like the pinpoints of light were . . . dancing.

Oh, why did the school have to have this dance?

It also seemed like there were two Caseys.

There was the no-nonsense Casey. The girl who didn't give a toad's butt about boys and dances. The journalist at large, thank you very much. The shy but tough girl who didn't want to trade her Converses for shiny dance shoes. The girl who wanted to stay a girl—not a woman. Not yet.

And then there was this other Casey. The girl who got all goofy when a boy named Tyler was around. The girl who had a china crack of curiosity about what it would be like to see the gym with the lights dimmed and music playing and everyone dealing with each other differently than we do in the locker halls. Maybe a dance could be fun.

If I had someone to go with.

I reached in my pack and pulled out my unopened box of juice. Nothing like a little O.J. to perk a girl up. One part fruit juice, zero parts carbonated sugar water. Feeling revived, I decided to concentrate on the survey. I needed to get this festering dance gunk out of my brain. A fester-free brain sounded good.

I was stuffing the empty juice box into my pack when Tyler appeared.

"Casey, why are you always on the ground?" he asked, looking down at me. It did seem like I was floor-surfing every time he came around.

I stood up, wiggling a little to get my backpack centered on my shoulders. "I was just, uh, conducting a science experiment."

"Really?" he asked, cracking his crooked-tooth smile.

I was going to say something really clever, but suddenly I lost my jokester train of thought. "Um, actually, no. I was just sitting here. Thinking about stuff. You know. Whatever."

He looked at me like I had just spoken Martian. I touched my hair, making sure I wasn't repeating Friday's rooster-do nightmare. Then I noticed the clipboard in my hand and held it out to him. "Here. *Real News* is doing a student survey on the Crush deal. Fill this out."

He grabbed the clipboard. "Got a pen?"

I watched him write:

Tyler McKenzie, grade 6: I say no way! School should be for learning, not for marketing to kids.

"Thanks," I said, taking back the clipboard. "You're the first person to respond."

"Great," he said. "Now you help me out," he said, flicking my shoulder. But it didn't hurt.

"How?" I asked, flicking his shoulder back.

"I've scored the fifty Zing T-shirts," he said, lowering his voice. "What I don't have is people to wear them. Any ideas?" He paused. "Actually, with you doing this survey thing . . . it's the perfect way to get the word out."

"Oh, right!" I said. "That's key. I can give a T-shirt to anyone who answers the poll with an anti-Crush quote."

"Exactly," he said, holding out his hand for a low five. "You know, we make a killer team."

I felt my stomach dip. I slapped his hand and said, "Okie-dokie!" regretting it the millisecond it flew out of my mouth. *Okie-dokie?*

"Hey I know those guys over there," he said, nodding at a group of kids playing hackey-sac. "Let's go ask them to do the survey."

"Um, okay," I said. We cruised over to them.

"Hey guys, can you stop for a minute and do a survey for the paper?" Tyler asked.

Everyone stopped. I was surprised to see how curious and excited they all were to get their name and quote in *Real News*.

Troy Chandler, grade 6: New cheerleader uniforms? I'll drink a case of Crush a day for that! I vote yes!

Melinda Puckett, grade 7: I think the idea is totally gross. I mean, you can press the Mute button on your remote for commercials on TV, but you can't mute Crush ads when they're in your face all day at school. I vote no.

Jenny Toledo, grade 8: I want to be a research biologist, so anything that gets new equipment for the labs is fine by me. YES!

Mark Allen, grade 7: Zing rules. Why don't we get Zing to donate money to the school?

Gonzo O'Maggio, grade 7: Ads are cool. Did you ever notice that sometimes the funniest part of a TV show is the ads?

Tyler and I spent the rest of lunch walking around getting quotes for the survey. We told the kids who were anti-Crush about the protest and when and where to get their shirts and cans of Zing Cola tomorrow morning.

Near the end of the period, we were standing under that huge tree, the one with the dancing leaves, counting how many quotes we had so far. We were pretty stoked at how many kids agreed to do the protest. Tyler was leaning over my shoulder looking at the clipboard, and I could smell the soap he used. Then my perfect lunch came to a screeching halt.

"Oh, hiii, Ty-lerrrr. . . ." Two voices at the same time. The Kelleher twins. One of the them was grinning at Tyler. Was it Keely? Or Kendall? Hard to tell. The other half was staring me down.

"It's the dynamic duo." Tyler was friendly. Too friendly? "Hey, you've got to do Casey's survey. What's your position on the Crush issue?"

"You *know* we can't stand the idea," one of them said.

"Okay," Tyler said, looking at me. "Keely Kelleher can't stand the idea." He pointed at my clipboard. "Write that down."

I was impressed that he could tell them apart.

"I think it's just awful," Kendall added. "You can put my quote down, too."

"Great. Thanks. How do you guys feel about joining our protest?" I asked.

"Oh, the protest," Kendall said. "I don't really want to walk around in one of those baggy shirts. Way too boyish for me."

"Ty-lerrr," Keely sang, stepping closer to him, "are you going to the dance?"

"I don't know." Tyler shrugged. "I haven't really thought about it. I've been into this Crush stuff."

"I was just wondering," she said, in that syrupy singsongy voice. "The dance is on Friday. After the protest is over. You won't be busy then, will you?"

Why didn't she just put a huge ASK ME! sign on her head?

"I guess not, but, um . . ." he said, not really looking at her. "Anyway, are you going to do the protest, even if Kendall doesn't?"

"Ugh." She rolled her eyes. "I'm not going to lug around a can of that Zing grossness all day." She grimaced. "I mean"—she suddenly got sweet again—"I detest Crush. But I don't really like Zing, either."

Can you say "Kiss up?"

I wished a big stinky wind would blow through and sweep the Kelleher clones to the other side of the schoolyard.

"Oh." Tyler looked sort of uncomfortable. It was so obvious that Keely wanted to go to the dance with him. Either he wasn't getting the hint, or he wasn't into Keely Kelleher.

"Maybe we could organize something else," Kendall said. "Like, maybe some focus groups?"

"Focus groups?" Tyler and I asked in unison. We looked at each other and yelped, "Jinx!" and then punched each other in the shoulder.

"Focus groups," Keely said really loudly, "are these important things they do in advertising. You get people together and show them ad campaigns. Then you ask them what they think. That's how companies know if one ad campaign is better than another."

She talked like a big know-it-all. Who cared about this stuff?

"If we did that here with the students, you

might be able to prove to Ms. Nachman exactly why no one likes the idea of Crush Cola being in the school. It's a media buy that the students don't want to buy in to," she droned on. And on. And on.

Was she trying to show off? Or was it just jabber to keep Tyler listening to her?

I needed to worm my way back into the conversation. "Wow, you sure know a lot about focus groups," I said, cutting her off in midsentence. "Where did you learn all that stuff?"

She gave me a stare as if I just asked her to scrape gum off my shoe. "I don't know, Casey. Definitely not in the same place you learned how to do square roots. And I know it wasn't in *Real News*."

"What's that supposed to mean?" I asked, blinking at her.

"Oh, nothing." She sniffed—a side effect from spending so much time looking down her nose. "I read a lot of things, that's where. Tyler"—she turned and was all smiles again—"you read a lot, don't you?"

I wanted to put a spell on her to grow a gigantic cyclops zit right between her eyes.

I couldn't stand here and watch this display of sugar and spice and everything gross. I started walking away.

"Hey Casey, where you going?" Tyler called after me.

"I gotta get going on this stuff," I said, turning and looking at him.

"Don't forget tomorrow." He smiled. I almost sighed—there was that crooked tooth again. But he didn't follow me.

It was official. Tyler was interested in Keely, the girl with half a birthday, half a wardrobe, half a bedroom and, if you ask me, half a brain. I was just his protest buddy. Then I thought about Griffin and Ringo and my brother, Billy. Yup. That's me: Casey Smith, a guy's best bud. Not a bad quality.

So why did I feel so awful?

Turn Your Recyclables Into Cold, Hard Art!

I MADE MY way to the *Real News* office and spread out all the surveys. Some people came up with really smart responses. Others just wrote stuff like, "Woo! Crush kicks butt!" But at least I had a lot of student opinions to help me out. I had also recruited people to meet Tyler and me tomorrow morning to get their Zing T-shirt, and protest.

I logged on to the Internet and started scanning web sites for any information on schools that had been sponsored by big corporations. I followed a link through a civil liberties organization and almost jumped up when I saw where it landed me. In Washington, there was a nonprofit organization dedicated to keeping schools from becoming giant billboards for big companies.

My newsnose went into overdrive.

According to all these formal studies, corporate sponsorship of public schools was back-door dealing with serious consequences that most teachers didn't even realize. And Crush Cola Company wasn't new to the idea of buying a campus. Take this one high school in Arizona. They were sponsored by Crush, but their promise of money had a catch. The students had to spend a certain amount of money for the soda in the machines and at games before Crush would actually fork over the promised cash. What a scam!

And there was more. The site said that companies wanted to build what the report called "label loyalty." That meant that they wanted to get kids hooked on a brand of soda so that they'd always buy that brand and not a competitor brand.

It was how they created customers for a lifetime!

But the only way to do that was to hook the customers while they were still kids. Being hooked on caffeine and sugar, the report said, could seriously hurt a kid's ability to learn, pay attention and in some cases, obey the rules. Heavy stuff.

There was also all kinds of stuff about how

half of the refined sugar that's consumed in the United States is in soda. I really had no idea that the average can of soda had twenty-three teaspoons of sugar. In Crush, there were twenty-eight teaspoons.

The last thing that caught my eye was the examples of schools that started with just a soda or candy sponsorship, but then more and more products were brought into the school. These schools practically became slaves to these slimy companies. From ads on the overhead projectors to textbook covers with pizza or candy logos, corporations totally took these schools over. But since the students didn't drink ten thousand cans of soda or eat three thousand candy bars a semester, they still didn't get their new football bleachers or whatever was promised.

Like new equipment for the science labs. Or computers for *Real News*.

I sat there in front of the old, slow computer with my jaw dropped. I just couldn't believe this.

I was printing out my findings when Ringo cruised into the office with a trippy-looking girl.

"C-C-C-Casey!" Ringo called. "What's going down? Besides Crush Cola?"

"Hey, Ringo," I said. This girl he was with looked as out of place as Ringo, but in a different way. She was pale and striking and, well, vampirish. Her skin was superfair, but it looked even lighter next to her all-black outfit. She was wearing leggings with heavy lace-up boots and a long T-shirt. She also wore a lot of silver jewelry. Her hair was jet black, and long, past her shoulders.

"Casey, allow me to introduce Ms. Melody Posen," Ringo said, bowing between us.

"Hello," Melody said. Her English accent made it sound like "Hellew!"

"Where are you from?" I asked.

"London," she said prettily. "I just moved here this last summer."

"Wow, London's a big city," I said. My parents had been there. They'd brought back a tiny statue of this clock called Big Ben. "It must be a shock coming to Dullsville, Massachusetts."

"Oh, Abbington is a bit small," she said. "But it's not land of the living dead or anything, is it?"

Land of the living dead?

"Melody's quite the pretty name, isn't it?" Ringo said, imitating her accent.

"Enough with that, Sir Ringo," she ordered, fixing him with a scary stare. Then she fixed her dark eyes on me. "Blame my mum for my ridiculous name. She was expecting a proper doll who would live for tea parties. I should think she's still surprised that I most enjoy sculpting. Especially sculptures based on the statues and engravings found in cemeteries and on large family tombs."

I didn't know if I should be freaked out or impressed. "I, uh, I know what you mean," I said. "I'm not the tea party type myself."

"Not exactly Mum's sweet little girl, what?" she added.

"What what?" Ringo asked.

"It's an English expression," she explained. "It's not Ringo lingo."

I decided that I liked this girl. She had the same no-nonsense attitude as Toni, but with a different accent. And style. Way different style.

"I had a sizzlin' idea," Ringo said. "Melody was showing me pictures of some sculptures she made in England."

"They were too large to cart overseas, you see." She sighed. "I was forced to leave my love-lies behind."

"She takes junk and puts it together to make it art," Ringo went on excitedly. "It's like recycling for art. Kind of. I mean, she takes total junk, and makes it beautiful."

"Well, I make it interesting," she said.

"So my idea was that after the protest, we could take the empty Zing cans and Melody could make them into one big sculpture," Ringo said, his arms stretched as wide as they could go.

"Look, I've done a sketch already." She pulled open her giant black satchel, which had practically a whole art supply store in it. There were two rows of markers lined up in color order, from the lightest yellow to the darkest black. There was a box of charcoal. Paintbrushes. And a couple of weird-looking tools. She pulled out a sketchbook that was covered in drawings of flying gargoyles and dragons, and opened to a sketch that looked sort of like a sinister bird made of little cylinder canisters.

It's *quite* lovely, I thought in my best British.

Ringo squatted down and beamed over the drawing. "I threw the idea out to Ms. Yablonski in the art department and she's all thumbs-up," Ringo said. "She even said she'd put it in the student art display case near the auditorium."

"I think that's a killer idea, you guys," I said. "It will remind students of their protest and their power, even after this whole Crush business is over."

"Quite," Melody said. "I'm so very glad you're not sitting by and letting them knock on your noggins without a fight," she went on. "Isn't it enough that corporations make those idiotic ads for the telly? I feel I could drive a stake through the hearts of those company executives this very minute."

Ringo made a dramatic gesture like he was just stabbed in the chest and then pretended to die a slow, tragic death. Melody took his hand and asked him to please look up her favorite dead uncle when he got to the "other side." That made Ringo laugh. I cracked a smile. This chick seemed to understand Ringo's fifth dimension.

"Hey dramazoids, I really like this idea of yours," I said. This girl was her own person, that was for sure. Her whole vampire, chick-of-the-night thing was sort of weird for my tastes, but to each her own, as Gram would say. And anyway, she was anti-Crush and willing to take an active part in helping us open students' eyes.

"Casey, you like it because it's brrrilliant!" Ringo said, taking a bow.

Melody smiled. "Ringo, you've had quite the brainstorm, haven't you?"

Ringo screwed his face up. "Not a storm. Just a minor squall," he reported. "It seems to be clearing up now."

"Hey, Ringy!" Samantha entered the office and waved to Ringo in this very lame cheerleader way. "We need you for a special cheer meeting. N-O-W now, dude!"

"Sam!" Ringo bolted toward the door. "Catch you guys later," he said, without even looking back. Then they disappeared around the corner.

I looked at Melody to see if she was as annoyed as I was that a cheerleader had just yanked Ringo away. And called him "Ringy." Melody had a look on her face all right, but it wasn't irritation. It was . . . what? It looked like major bummage. Could it be that this tough gothic English girl had a soft spot for my freaky-deaky Ringo?

"Hello, stranger!"

Gram was in the kitchen when I got home, which is weirder than it sounds. Gram doesn't know what to do with herself in a kitchen. Her idea of cooking is stirring something halfway through its seven minutes in the microwave. A habit possibly learned from living in New York City and ordering lots of takeout.

She was puzzling over a canister of instant biscuits.

"How the heck do these work?" she quizzed me. "Do I just put the whole thing in the oven?"

I took the canister from her and whacked it on the edge of the counter. It gave a satisfying *pop*, and the dough inside squidged out. I got out a round pan and started putting the soft raw dough pats into it.

"What's up, Betty Crocker?" I asked, setting the temperature on the oven.

Gram sighed and riffled her short hair with one hand. It's sort of multishine: red with streaks of gold and silver. "I'm procrastinating," she admitted. "I was working on my book and I hit a knotty part. I just couldn't stare at that computer anymore. So I'm making up excuses not to work."

"Now I know where I get it from," I teased.

"Ha ha, junior," she said, watching me put the pan in the oven as if I was launching the space shuttle. "So what's going on at school?"

I pulled out my copy of *Real News* from my backpack. Since I rarely do editorials, I'd sort of saved it as a surprise. "Gram, you have to read my editorial. Mr. Baxter said it went too far and that it was way over the line. But it got a lot of people fired up. One student even vandalized the new Crush machines, and Ms. Nachman called me into her office. But I remembered all the things you told me about the media, and she listened to me. But tomorrow there's going to be a student protest, and—"

Gram held up her hand, which meant "Slow down, Casey." She holds up her hand a lot. Then she told me to get out the milk while she read my editorial. She sat down and read, and a frown creased her brow. I knew not to be worried by that, though. She always frowns when she's concentrating.

"Over the line?" she asked, when she finished reading. "No. Definitely not. If this were a news article, Mr. Baxter might have a point saying it was biased and coming on too strong. But this is an editorial. It's supposed to give an opinion. And make people want to react. Oh, and you did a good job, by the way."

"Thanks, Gram." A compliment on my writing from Gram had a lot of weight. "So why do you think he got so upset about it?"

"Well, Casey, he is the advisor for *Real News*," she pointed out. "He was probably getting a lot of heat about your editorial from the administration."

"Yeah, I guess." I was a little bummed that Mr. Baxter would cave so easily. But I guessed I could see Gram's point.

"You know, I used to hate the fact that they'd show commercials during the news on TV," Gram said thoughtfully. "It just seemed wrong that one second you'd see an anchorperson talking about homes being bombed in Northern Ireland, and then the next second switch to a happy family eating some brand of popcorn. But you've got to keep in mind that those ads pay the bills. If that popcorn company didn't buy that air time, we probably wouldn't get to see the news at all."

"I think I get that," I said. "But what does that have to do with Crush crushing our freedom of choice?"

"The companies that buy air time don't tell the news programs what to do," Gram explained. "Maybe Crush wouldn't be as invasive a force as you think. The bottom line, somebody has to pay the bills. Sometimes it's the parent-teacher groups. Sometimes there are federal grants. But it's not easy. Lots of schools are crunched for dollars."

Then I told Gram about the research I had dug up that afternoon. About how some companies that buy out schools *do* tell the schools what to do—or else they won't give them the promised money. I also told her all that stuff about label loyalty and getting kids hooked early. She listened to me, tapping her fingers on the table and staring at me thoughtfully.

"Gram, I mostly just want to know what to do next," I said as the oven dinged. I took out the biscuits and poked one. They had baked to a perfect light brown. "If only this thing with Crush was as easy as instant biscuits. Follow the directions and get exactly what you want."

"What you do next is follow your gut instincts," she said. "It sounds like you're convinced corporate sponsorship in school is a bad idea. So study your research, consider all the different angles and write a good, solid story. Trust people to draw their own conclusions. If you're right, they'll look at the evidence and agree with you."

"Uh, yeah, that'll be easy to do," I said, slumping. "I'll just go whip that story up right now."

"Welcome to journalism, dearie," she said, matching my sarcasm. "But listen—that's my professional advice. As for my personal advice, I say when you're not acting as a journalist you can be as opinionated as you want. Didn't you mention something about a protest?"

"Yes!" I grinned. "And I'm in."

"Work it, Casey," Gram cheered. "Fight the power!"

Student Protest
Crushed by Crush!

GROUND ZERO. WEDNESDAY morning. Operation Crush
Crush is about to begin.

A bunch of boys were whacking a handball
against the brick wall outside the gym. I spotted
Tyler across the parking lot, and he waved me
over like a spy on assignment.

I wanted to run, but I didn't want to draw
attention. Talk about stomach butterflies!

"Hey, Case, you made it," Tyler said, extending
his palm for a low five.

"Hey, Ty, got the goods?" I asked, slapping his
hand.

"Check 'em out." He held up in one hand an
orange T-shirt with a royal-blue ZING! across the
front and in the other, a matching can of soda.
"We've got three boxes of shirts. Not bad, huh?"

127

"What's up, you guys?" Jen Simon, a seventh-grade member of student government, turned the corner with three friends. "Is that the stuff?"

Within the next few minutes, a steady flow of anti-Crush students began showing up at our designated outpost next to the gym. Tyler and I were totally in synch, passing out T-shirts to our posse of protesters. As Tyler pulled them out, I handed one to a customer. It was their choice if they wanted to drink a can of the soda, which we also had several cartons of.

"Look, I wore matching tights," Jen Simon said, kicking her legs like a karate master. Her leggings were the same blue as the Zing logo.

"Nice," I said. "It's important to have a color-coordinated revolution."

I took another look at the Zing logo when I handed out the next shirt. There was something strange about it. But what? Then I realized it was slightly different from the one I was used to seeing. It was sort of rounded, three-dimensional, as if someone had taken the old logo and given it a slick new update.

The slogan was different, too. Usually, it was "Zingin' in the . . ." whatever. Like, the first commercial was "Zinging' in the rain," and then it branched out to "Zingin' in the sun," "in the snow," "on the beach," whatever. Totally stupid, right? Except apparently it worked, seeing how I remembered it so well.

Anyway these T-shirts had a different slogan: "SomeZing for everyone."

"That's weird," I said to Tyler as he broke down the last empty box for the recycling bin. "These don't look like any Zing slogans I've ever seen."

He just shrugged and handed me a pile. I held them out to the next pair of waiting hands. Off to my right, Dave Sherman and Tom Turvey were both pulling their shirts off. They had "Crush Crush!!!" written in blue paint on their chests.

"Uh, guys? Is that really necessary?" I asked.

"WOOOOOO-EEEE!" they whooped, and whipped their new Zing shirts above their heads as they headed to the school's front lawn. This was definitely going to be a crazy morning.

Then I saw my two favorite people, the Kelleher twins, get out of a fancy car and walk toward the outpost.

"Hiii Tyyy-lerrrr. . . ." No mistake which one was Keely this time.

I shoved a T-shirt directly between Keely's face and Tyler's. "Here, join in the reindeer games," I said.

"No, thank you," Keely said, as if I had just

offered her a seat at the opera.

"But they are lovely shirts," Kendall added.

"So why don't you put one on and help us out?" I asked again.

"I *said*, no, thank you," Keely repeated with pinched lips.

Just then there was a frantic honking from the street, and I saw a red-haired man in a car waving two identical lunchbags out the window.

"Girls!" he hollered. "You forgot your lunches!"

"We'd better get those, Kee-Kee . . ." Kendall started.

"Or we'll have to eat Mrs. Stekol's giant meatballs!" Keely finished.

"Yuck!" They heebie-geebied together and took off toward the car. Why I noticed that I'd never seen their dad before, I'll never know. Maybe because their mom always drops them off. At least now I know where they got that flaming red hair.

"Well, Casey, that's it," Tyler announced.

We were ready to rock.

Dressed in our orange-and-blue Zing T-shirts and toting orange cans of soda, our posse met on the front steps of the school. We walked into the front doors of Trumbull in a large orange cluster. The plan was to enter school together, go to our homerooms, then meet up between classes to march through the halls.

I counted the crew as we moved through the sixth-grade locker hall. There were just over fifty of us. Not too shabby.

As the first homeroom bell sounded, I looked over at Tyler. He gave me the two-finger peace sign. I gave it back, and we went our separate ways.

The protest was about to begin.

In homeroom, the speaker above the black-board crackled, and then I heard Ms. Nachman's voice. It was crackling, too . . . with anger.

"Students, the vandal or vandals who destroyed the vending machines have struck again," she announced in a stiff voice. "This time, they have destroyed the new team uniforms by cutting out the Crush logo. This is unacceptable behavior!"

Her voice was like a jackhammer pounding through the speaker.

"Whoever you are," Ms. Nachman's voice hissed, "you may have gotten away with this so far. But rest assured, you will be caught. This school has zero tolerance for vandalism. Anyone with any information about this vandal, please come see me. That is all."

The room erupted with chatter. I could not believe someone was this hard-core. Peaceful protest, yes. But what was the point of ruining stuff?

"The Crusher struck again!" one kid said, high-fiving his friend.

The Crusher? Now this horrible person had a name?

Some kids seemed to think this was the greatest thing since video games. Other kids seemed really freaked out that there was a meanie among us. The fact that I was wearing a Zing T-shirt made some of my classmates glare at me suspiciously. I shrank down in my seat.

The Crusher was biting off my piece of glory. I'd love to catch that creep. The homeroom final bell finally sounded. It was time to make our first move.

We gathered by the front doors, then marched down the main hallway of the school. The Crush representatives had arrived and were in front of the main office, handing out their corporate stuff. Plenty of kids were lined up for their free loot. It's not like we could stop anyone from doing that. But as we strode down the hall, all eyes turned to look at us.

We were chanting, "Crush, Crush, down with Crush!" as we moved slowly through the school. Some students were guzzling Zing Cola and holding up anti-Crush signs. Others were just drinking

Diet Cool and O.K. Cola. It was such a rush to be a part of something bigger than just one person. Something that could change the way people think.

The reps from Crush glared at us like we were from Planet Zing. But they looked like kittens next to Ms. Nachman, whose face was like a mascaraed thundercloud. She stood like a rock with her fists firmly set against her hips. It was a sight, considering she happened to be wearing a frilly lemon-yellow suit.

Our march lasted all of eight minutes. But it felt like we'd marched to Washington or something. Score one for our side!

When the bell rang, we disbanded to go to class. I was making my way to my locker when Gary cruised up.

"Hey, Casey," he said. "I got some info I think you'll find mighty useful." He handed me a folded piece of notebook paper. It was a list of the people who had access to the coach's office. People who could get in there and cut the logos out of the new uniforms. People who might be the vandal.

"Gar. You rule!" I said, checking out the list. "How'd you—?"

"Simple deduction, my dear Watson. You

spend enough time on teams and in locker rooms and pretty soon you know who could get in and who couldn't," he said, getting a little macho. He always does that when he talks about sports. Even though he's always second string. "But there's a problem."

"Oh great. What?" I moaned. Why isn't anything easy?

"The coach's office was unlocked yesterday during second period," he said. "I talked to him, and he said he left it open because they were replacing his old file cabinets with bigger ones. That means this list includes everyone who had second-period gym."

I looked at it. It was long. Lots of football players and cheerleaders were on it. Most of them were pro-Crush because they wanted new uniforms.

Then there were the class rosters for second-period gym. I went through and checked off all the pro-Crushers. There were actually a lot of people I knew on the list. Tyler, the Kelleher twins, Ringo and his new friend-of-the-night, Melody.

After I eliminated all the pro-Crush people, I was left with a medium-sized list of people who were either undecided or anti-Crush. None of them seemed that suspicious to me. Samantha, the hypoglycemic cheerleader with her Diet Cool habit? I couldn't picture her taking scissors to the football uniforms, but anything was possible.

I stared at the paper full of names. How was I supposed to narrow the list down?

"Oh, good, Casey, you're here," Megan greeted me as I came into the *Real News* office at lunch. She was sitting beside Toni, holding up a magazine.

"Sorry I'm late," I said. "I wanted to get a few more poll answers."

"Oh, forget about the poll," Megan scoffed. "I just want to know what you think of this outfit." She shoved the magazine in front of me and pointed to a dress on a model. "It's kind of different for me, with the long, swirly skirt. Do you think it'd look like I was trying too hard?"

I looked. I saw. I shrugged. I guess it was an all-right dress, but who really wore stuff like that?

"Megan, have you noticed that Ringo would wear a dress before I would?" I asked, scratching my armpit. It was hot today, and I had on two T-shirts. "Why are you asking me?"

Megan picked up the magazine, disappointed.

"It's just that Toni said she likes it, but I think she's just being nice," she said. "I know you'd never spare my feelings."

"Well," I said, smirking, "you got me there." I dumped my bag on Dalmatian Station. Toni barely looked up from her slouching position at the table. "Anyway, Megan," I said, "why put all this time and energy into spending two or three hours in a dark gym? Do you really care so much about this dance?"

Megan tossed her magazine down onto the table. "Honestly, Casey, would it kill you to just stop putting the dance down? Why shouldn't people have a little fun?"

"You call that fun?" I snorted. "Puh-lease. I have better things to do with my time."

"Oh, really?" Toni asked, smacking her gum and raising a perfect brown eyebrow at me. "Like what?"

"Like watching paint dry," I snapped back. "I think I might even pick the scuzz out from between my toes if I can fit it in with all my other glamorous activities."

The truth was I didn't have anything better to do. Especially since every kid I knew was going to be busy at that stupid dance. I didn't even have a group of buddies to go with. Toni was going with her group. Gary was going with the sports guys. Megan would probably go with Mr. Suck-up Spence. And Ringo was going to take a fellow rah-rah.

So that's when I decided to develop a bad cold just before the dance. I could start coughing on Friday afternoon. And then on Monday I could tell everyone it got worse and worse until going to a dance was simply against doctor's orders.

Perfect. I wouldn't have to go to the dance. And, better, I wouldn't have to go alone.

"Well, I wish I was as sophisticated as you," Megan said. "I guess us simple folk will just have to make do with our dumb old dance this Friday. You can pick at your toes in peace, Mademoiselle Casey."

"Whoa, I'm feeling funky vibes," Ringo said, coming into the office.

"Casey's just being a big old grump about the dance again," Toni said as she inspected the rings on her fingers.

"Oh. The dance." Ringo sank into a chair.

"Hey, Ringo! Where's your Zing T-shirt?" I demanded.

He looked at me with puppy eyes. "Samantha got upset about the uniforms being ruined, so she dropped out of the protest. She thinks it's gone too far. Now she's pro-Crush."

"Which means you just had to drop out of the protest then?" I asked. "I can't believe you, Ringo!"

"I know, I know," Ringo moaned. "I was all Zing, all the time. I swear. But every time I see Samantha, I just forget there ever was a Zing. She comes around and I'm like, 'Zing who?' Sam zaps my Zing and it seems unimportant. I become Zingless. A Zing-free dude."

"Unimportant?" I meant to yell, but it came out a whisper. "What's more important than saving our school from being a tool of some money-grubbing corporation?"

Ringo adjusted the bandanna on his head. "I know it sounds dumb," he said. "But it's the dance. I have to ask Samantha today or some other dude is going to snag her. And if I'm a Zinger, she might say no."

"Poor Ringo." Megan gave him a soothing pat on the shoulder. "Don't listen to Casey. You go ahead and ask her, and don't sweat the other stuff."

Ringo brightened a little. "I figured out how I'm going to do it," he said, pulling out a piece of sketch paper with a Simon cartoon. "I'm having Simon pop the question."

"While he's at it, have him ask where your brain went when it leaked out your ears," I sniped.

SIMON SAYS—CHECK ONE

☐ Yes, I will go to the dance with you!

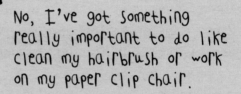

☐ No, I've got something really important to do like clean my hairbrush or work on my paper clip chair.

"Not to mention your loyalty. And your priorities."

"Casey, just leave him alone," Megan ordered. "Just because you don't want to go to the dance doesn't mean you should expect Ringo to not go. This is a big deal for some people."

I grabbed my backpack and was about to leave when the speaker on the wall made its usual crackling sound.

"Students, I have a quick announcement," Ms. Nachman's voice echoed. "In light of the recent vandalism, and after receiving a disturbing call from the Crush representatives, I have made a decision. There have been confrontations with Zing protesters, and the Crush people do not appreciate this. They took it as a sign that Trumbull Middle School is not interested in accepting their funding."

"Yes!" I said, throwing my fist in the air. "We are Trumbull! Hear us roar!"

Ms. Nachman's voice continued: "So I now have no choice but to forbid students to wear clothing with logos from Zing or any rival soda company. I cannot have a small minority ruining things for the rest of the students. Students with Zing or any other rival company T-shirts will face serious punishment. Effective immediately."

She clicked off.

"She can't do that!" I wailed. "That's not legal!" I wheeled around and faced Ringo, Megan and Toni. "Don't you see what's happening?" They just stared back at me. "Don't you?" They looked at each other, then back at me. Nothing. No reaction at all.

I yanked my backpack onto my shoulder and stormed out.

I knew Tyler had lunch at the same time I did. I found him at his locker. His Zing shirt was slung over his arm.

"What could I do?" he asked. "I mean, is it worth getting suspended?"

I glanced down at my Zing shirt. Was this it? Time to jump ship? "But she can't tell us what to wear!" I insisted. "Can she? I mean, it's not legal! Is it?"

Tyler shrugged. "Break school rules and what happens?"

"Serious punishment," Ms. Nachman had said.

"But it's not fair," I said.

"Casey, we've lost this battle. But the war isn't over." He was right.

Slowly, I pulled my Zing T-shirt off and stuffed it into my pack. Did I have a choice? I felt like a horrible fraud, standing there in my plain, regular shirt.

"What a massive drag," I said.

"Yeah, massive," Tyler said. "If we don't keep the protest going, everyone will just cave to the Crush deal. There has to be another way to fight this."

He was looking to me for the answer. And I didn't want to let him down. I fished out my empty can of Zing and rolled it around in my palm like it was a genie's magic lamp. My brain was totally empty. As empty as this can. This empty, empty can . . .

I grabbed Tyler's arm and pulled him close.

"Tyler," I whispered in his ear. "I have an idea."

CHAPTER 14

War Declared Between Crushers and Zingers!

DATELINE: Wednesday, last period.

LOCATION: An empty art room. (So I was supposed to be in the library working on my Spanish project—a greeting card. Hasta la vista, Crush!)

PLAN OF ACTION: Operation Crush Crush limps on.

PLAYERS: Casey, Tyler, Melody

We weren't about to be brought down by Ms. Nachman's latest illegal orders. School is such a dictatorship!

Tyler and I were sitting at a long green table

with Melody. Empty cans of Zing were all around us. Melody drew a series of shapes on paper, which Tyler and I used as patterns. Cutting with these heavy-duty industrial scissors, we cut the aluminum cans into small pieces.

My plan was to make jewelry out of the empty Zing cans. But we needed Melody's help.

"Take care now to keep the logo in the middle of the shape," Melody ordered in her very British way. "We want people to see what the jewelry is made of, don't we?"

"This was a great idea," Tyler said, concentrating on his cutting. "You really came up with a whopper this time, Casey."

I shrugged like I didn't care, but inside I was about to burst. "I just remembered that Melody knew how to make sculpture out of aluminum cans," I said. "I figured if she could do that, she could make jewelry."

"And what a loophole," Tyler said, then gave his best maniac laugh. "Ms. Nachman said we couldn't wear clothes with a rival logo. She didn't say anything about jewelry."

I grinned at my fellow revolutionary. I was tempted to hum a little tune as I cut out my triangle.

"How many have you there, Miss Casey?" Melody asked. "Pass them over to me, thank you."

She carefully curled back the edges, rolling them around a narrow stick so they wouldn't cut anything. Then she poked holes in the corners with a sharp tool she said was usually used for leather-working. Finally, she took fishing line and strung the pieces together.

"That is amazing," I said. The necklace was definitely eye-catching. The pieces were about as big as the palm of my hand, so there was no missing them. At the same time, the necklace actually looked funky. Almost stylish.

"That's quite nice, but I think I'll string a few singles to get things rolling," Melody said.

I pulled the first necklace over my head as she got to work on the next one. "Now, this is fashion I can care about," I announced.

"As opposed to what?" Tyler asked.

"For the last week everyone has been so obsessed with the dance and whether they're wearing floral or fluorescents," I told him, rolling my eyes.

"Not into it?" he asked, concentrating on his can.

"What am I going to wear? Should I go to the mall? Should I get this outfit? Oooohhhh. . . ." I imitated Megan and Toni.

Tyler and Melody both laughed.

"Yes, right, I know what you mean," Melody

said, working quickly to finish another necklace. "It's especially awful when all the good fellows seem to want to go with, what's the word you use? Cheesy girls?"

"Yeah, Mel, cheesy is exactly right." I seethed, thinking of Kee-Kee-Keely, the chee-chee-cheesiest of them all. "I don't know what happens to guys. It's like their brains empty out as soon as you say the word *dance*."

"Well"—Tyler seemed very busy with his can-cutting—"I don't know. I don't think it's just the guys."

"Okay, you're right about that," I agreed. "The girls get stupid, too. Everybody's got Dance Flu. People would rather talk about long skirts versus miniskirts than deal with their school becoming a communist regime."

"Right again," Melody chimed in. "And they prefer to have those chats with cheerleaders rather than artists, don't they?"

"Um . . . yeah," I agreed. Melody and Ringo. It confirmed what I'd picked up on earlier. But from what I'd seen, Ringo was still not getting it. "This dance is just lame from beginning to end."

"Casey?" Tyler said, looking at me all serious.

What could be that serious? I dodged his dark eyes with a joke. "Yes, what is it, thank you," I said in an attempt to sound like Melody.

She grinned without looking up from her task.

Tyler handed me a cutting tool. "Get back to work, will you?"

We finished with the necklaces and hit the locker halls after the last bell. I couldn't believe what a huge hit the jewelry was! As soon as people saw the metallic goods, they started grabbing at them like loose dollar bills. I was really surprised at how many students weren't afraid of Ms. Nachman's threats. I thought we would've lost a lot more people to the Crusher's latest act of vandalism, but there were plenty of Zingers left.

Tomorrow, the Zingers take back the school!

Three Crushes—Girl Reporter
Strikes Out!

THE NEXT MORNING I was proudly wearing my Zing necklace, ready to hold my head high in the halls of Trumbull. But the minute I walked in the front doors, I found out I was not taking a popular stand.

The message scrawled in the front foyer shrieked from the shiny tiles:

CRUSH, GO HOME!

The Crusher had struck again.

This time it wasn't small-fry stuff like damaging the vending machines. Or even cutting the uniforms. This time it was scary.

Throughout the school, in classrooms and

hallways, walls were covered with anti-Crush graffiti. In bright purple ink, the Crusher's hatefulness was everywhere:

GET OUT OF OUR FACES, CRUSH!

CRUSH: SMELLS LIKE SLUSH,
TASTES LIKE MUSH

And the graffiti was just the beginning. The Crusher had also taken all the soda that the Crush reps had left behind—cans and cans of the stuff—and dumped it all over the girls' locker room. The floor was a rainbow-colored, super-sticky river. And the ants had already come marching in.

The halls were a loud chorus of Crusher gossip.

It was ugly and awful. I didn't like Crush, but I also knew this vandalism was wrong. I didn't want my school destroyed. I liked my school. That's why I was doing everything I could to stop the Crush takeover. But the Crusher totally missed the point. At this rate, we were going to be worse off than before Crush.

I'd barely made it into the building when I spotted Ms. Nachman stomping down the hall. The vice principal and two of the office ladies were right behind her, taking orders and looking scared out of their wits. Ms. Nachman practically had smoke coming out of her nostrils.

I shrank back. Like I really needed her to see me in my Zing jewelry and blame me for this latest catastrophe.

"Call the superintendent and tell him what's happened," I heard her bark. "Let him know I'm canceling gym classes. The girls' locker room is a mess. And he should get over here, pronto."

For a half second I forgot I was scared. No gym? Bonus! But then Ms. Nachman hollered something else to be done and continued with her ranting all the way through the hall and into the next one. "I want this vandal found!" I heard her screech.

I touched my necklace.

Suddenly I felt very nervous. My funky jewelry suddenly seemed too big, too obvious and too anti-Crush. People were looking at me and the shiny Zing logos around my neck. And glaring. Like they thought that everyone who didn't want Crush in the school was a vandal.

Then it hit me.

Where were all the necklaces I passed out the day before? I saw a few of the kids who took one, but not one of them was wearing their anti-Crush jewelry. Did Ms. Nachman have them all running scared? Or were they afraid to be tied to the Crusher?

I definitely felt like I was wearing a clown costume at a wedding.

Hold your head high, I told myself. I knew what I was doing was right. It wasn't my fault that the Crusher was clueless about how to change things in a peaceful and positive way. Moving down the hall I silently repeated, You believe in this, Casey. Just keep walking.

With my jaw set and my eyes fixed straight ahead, I headed for my locker. And it was like I had student repellent on. Kids would look at the necklace, then step away like it had scary laser powers and was about to burn their eyeballs out of their sockets.

Then I saw Tyler.

There he was, cool as a fresh-from-the-machine can of soda, leaning against a locker. The long chain necklace with the Zing pendant hung over his white cotton shirt. Standing out.

I wasn't alone.

"Casey!" He waved me over.

I beat a path through the stragglers in the hall.

"Fight the power, dudette," he said to me with a sideways grin.

"Are we the only ones?" I asked, touching my jewelry.

"Looks that way. I haven't seen anyone else."

I smiled at him. Then I felt dumb. So I looked away really fast and tugged at my backpack straps. Then I remembered something. "Hey, wait!" I belted out. "What about Melody? I know she's wearing her own creation."

Tyler put his hands in his pockets. "Oh, yeah. She called me last night and said she came down with something. Stomach flu or something. She sounded really bad. I don't think she's coming to school today."

"Oh." I felt a little more air rush out of my protest balloon.

"She said she was really sorry," Tyler said.

But my nose was itching. I thought about yesterday and how into this whole thing Melody was. Funny, she didn't have any symptoms of being sick yesterday. And then it came to me: In Melody's satchel, the satchel that was like an art store, I'd seen markers. Thick ones. In every color.

Including bright purple.

Could Melody be the Crusher? Could she be the vandal who was destroying my school? And did she stay home today so no one would suspect her?

I pulled my backpack off and fished out my notebook. I flipped to the page where I had copied down the names of the people who had access to the coach's office. Sure enough, there was Melody: second-period gym.

"Casey, what are you doing?" Tyler asked.

But before I could explain to him, Toni sauntered up to us.

"Leave it to you, girl," she said, pulling out her camera. "You know how to make trouble, don't you? I definitely have to get the rebellious couple on film."

Couple? I stared right at Toni like I was hypnotized.

Tyler put his arm around me and did a thumbs-up sign. I could barely breathe, so I just smiled weakly and did a thumbs-up sign, too.

"Not so fast!" an angry voice called from behind us.

Toni slowly lowered her camera and looked down the hall. "Uh-oh. Ms. Nachman."

"Casey Smith! Turn around!" the principal ordered.

Tyler and I swung around. Ms. Nachman looked so mad, I thought she was going to vaporize me with her glare. Tyler squeezed my elbow.

It was like slow motion. She strode over. She checked out our necklaces. Then reached over and yanked Toni's camera out of her hands.

"Excuse me?" Toni said, her head bobbing. "That would be my property."

"Yes, well, Ms. Velez, you're using it on school property," Ms. Nachman said, holding the camera up like a roasted pig on a platter. "And I'm confiscating it. I don't want this film made into photos."

"Excuse me?" Toni said with her hands on her hips. "This school is not the only place where I take pictures. I've got stuff on this roll that has nothing to do with the place. Like my sister's birthday party." Didn't I tell you she was fearless? "Besides, I buy that film myself, Ms. Nachman."

"Well. You should have thought of that before."

"Before what?" Toni demanded. She was about to get in trouble. And this was my battle.

"Ms. Nachman, I think—"

"As for you," Ms. Nachman interrupted me. "And you, Mr. McKenzie. You two come with me."

We stared at her.

"Now!" she barked, pointing at the floor.

We both jumped. And started walking. Did we have another option? Dread hung over my head like an indoor storm cloud. I didn't think we had done anything wrong. But my Zing jewelry felt

heavy and loud. It clinked and clanked conspicu-
ously as we walked down the hall.

I snuck a glance at Tyler, and he winked at me.

We both sat down in front of Ms. Nachman's
desk and waited for her to start yelling or call our
parents or the National Guard or *something*.

It seemed like she spent years frowning at the
blotter on her desk. Finally, she looked up at us
and folded her hands. "The last thing this school
needs is you two provoking an already bad situation."

"We have the right to express our opinions,"
I said, leaning forward. "We're just—"

"You're just making things worse, Casey," she
interrupted, giving me a look that said "You'll
speak when I say you speak."

"The safety of my students is compromised
right now," she continued. "This is gravely serious, Casey. I need you to do as I say and obey my
rules."

We were quiet for a minute. It felt like an hour.

"Do either of you know who the vandal is?"

"No!" We both answered at once. We looked
at each other and stifled a laugh. A silent jinx
moment.

"What's so funny?" Ms. Nachman demanded.
But just then her secretary beeped in and told
her she needed her in the front office.

"I'll be right back. Don't move," she ordered and left the room.

"This is way better than English class," Tyler said.

I grinned at him. Then I had a thought. Could the actual Crush contract be somewhere in this room? On this desk? I stared at the neat desk and the files stacked on the cabinet behind it.

"Tyler, watch the door for me, will you?" I slipped my backpack off and slunk to the other side of Ms. Nachman's desk.

"Casey, what are you doing?" Tyler was on the edge of his seat looking from me to the door to me to the door.

"Just looking. Do you think there's a copy of the Crush contract here?"

He almost jumped off the chair. "Are you crazy?"

"Maybe. Probably."

But I didn't care. My newsnose was on fire. I just knew that contract was here. And I wanted to find out exactly what Crush demanded of Trumbull students before it would cough up the promised money.

The desktop was spotless. A plant in an ugly pot. Some pictures of a little boy in a baby pool. Toni's camera, the phone and a pad of paper. Then I turned to the rack of files on the cabinet.

Sort of a grate that held a dozen or so files upright. Organized, labeled files.

Jackpot?

I sifted through them.

"Casey! Come on!" Tyler called from the door, where he was peeking through the crack.

"Shhhh!" I bared my teeth at him. Then I held up a file and grinned. "Exhibit A, Mr. McKenzie. The Crush file."

He blinked at it like it was a bright light.

I slapped it on the desk, opened it and started reading furiously. It was confusing and stodgy. But then I found this section about "student involvement."

"Okay, they require that only Crush soda machines be placed in 'key' spots throughout campus," I whispered loudly. "And if the students don't drink twenty thousand cases of soda by the end of this year, we won't get new science equipment!"

Twenty thousand!

The contract said that amounted to "only" about forty dollars per student per year. Per student! Like there was a price on our heads!

"And listen to this," I went on. "If we don't agree to advertising in halls *and* classrooms, they're not going to repair the gym!"

I was only on page three of a very thick contract, and already I had found tight strings attached to the deal. Trumbull was about to get majorly ripped off, and this proved it.

Too bad I didn't have a minicamera stashed in the heel of my shoe to take pictures of this contract. Casey Smith, international spy girl!

"Casey," Tyler whispered like a lunatic and jumped to his chair. "Ms. Nachman!"

I dropped the contract, replaced the folder, bolted around the desk and practically dove into my chair. My heart was pounding when Ms. Nachman walked in.

"Okay you two, back to business." Ms. Nachman went around her desk and sat down. She looked at me for a long second. Was I sweating?

"Ms. Nachman," Tyler said, "we don't know who the vandal is. We laughed because we jinxed each other and—"

"It doesn't matter," she interrupted him. "As of this moment, you are both suspended."

The word hung in the air like fish odor.

Suspended.

As if we had been caught cheating. Or smoking. My mouth dropped open, but I was too shocked to speak.

"For two days. And I'm sure you realize that when you are suspended you miss more than class," Ms. Nachman continued. "You are barred from all school activities. Including *Real News*," she said, shooting a look at me. Then she turned to Tyler. "And, of course, the dance."

I wedged my black Converse against the foot of Ms. Nachman's desk. This was unfair. And I wasn't going to take it.

Casey Smith, girl reporter, was not going down without a fight.

Boy Hero Has Skeletons in His Locker!

I HELD UP my hands, as if the only way to stop Ms. Nachman was to motion like a traffic cop. "This is wrong," I said firmly. "You're suspending us for—for what? Wearing homemade jewelry?"

Ms. Nachman shook her head. "You know it's much worse than that, Casey. You and Tyler are trying to rile up the students. I've already got a vandal destroying school property. I don't need you two egging him or her on."

Whoa! Like we were the hands working the vandal puppet. "So what are you telling us?" I pressed. "That we shouldn't have an opinion? That we can't get the word out to kids when something wrong is happening in our school?"

"In this case, that's exactly what I'm saying," Ms. Nachman said crisply. "I warned you about this, Casey. I want you to back off from this Crush thing. Today. And if I have to suspend you to make my point, so be it."

I couldn't believe what I was hearing. "Have you ever heard of the First Amendment?" I said, rising up like an angry pirate. "What about my freedom of speech? Are you going to ban me from talking?"

Ms. Nachman rose to look me in the eye. "Let's not exaggerate. You'll understand this when you get older, Casey. Kids don't always have the same rights as adults."

She sat back down and let out a breath. Dismissing us. "Now go get your things. Both of you."

Tyler looked stunned as he stood up beside me.

I wanted to scream and yell and pound my fists on her desk. But what was the point? Had she heard anything I had said?

"Go directly to your lockers and pack *all* of your books," Ms. Nachman went on. "You will still get homework. This is not a vacation. Then come back to the administrative office."

As we walked out of the office, I wondered how I was going to explain this to Gram. Had we really gone too far?

"I'm stunned," Tyler said. "And my dad is going to freak."

"I was just thinking the exact same thing," I said. "Gram supported this whole protest thing. But I don't think she expected me to get suspended. And no *Real News*—"

"My parents were behind me, too," Tyler said. "I know they didn't think I'd get kicked out of school. But I still think we're doing the right thing."

"Oh, me too! I know we were right to stand up to Crush, and to Ms. Nachman. The students should know about a deal this big. And we should have a vote."

"Yes!" Tyler said and bumped my hip with his hip.

"Do that again and I'll be forced to put you in a headlock," I said, giving him my most serious face.

"Oh, right! I'd like to see you try." He cracked a smile. "Hey, how about if I go with you to your locker and you come with me to mine?"

"Okay," I said. We were talking and laughing, but it was a cover.

"Suspended," Tyler said when we got to my locker. He ran a hand through his hair. "Um, I gotta ask you something."

I finished the combination but I didn't open it.

"You're not upset with me for getting you into all this, are you?" he said, shifting from one foot to the other. But before I could even answer he kept going.

"I read your editorial and I thought you were right," he went on. "I wanted to do something." He glanced at me. "I'm sorry for all this."

I didn't know what to say.

So I socked him in the shoulder.

"Does that mean we're cool then?" he asked, rubbing his arm.

"I don't know what you're talking about," I said, grabbing my books and stuffing them into my pack. "You didn't get me into anything."

"But it was my idea," he said. "I feel like I got us both in trouble."

"Tyler, zip it!" I said, grabbing at my Zing necklace. "I knew the risk, and I went for it. I make up my own mind."

"That's for sure," he answered.

I thought he was kidding. But one flash of his brown eyes and I knew he wasn't. He admired me. *Me*. This was one roller coaster of a day.

I slammed my locker shut and we started walking.

"I'm really sorry we'll miss the dance," he said as we rounded the corner to his locker.

"Oh, that dumb thing," I scoffed. "I'm not missing anything. I would never have gone in a million years. Ms. Nachman just gave me the excuse I needed."

"Really?" He sounded disappointed. "You think it'll be a bust?"

I was about to assure him that the dance was lame when a light flashed on in my brain: Was Tyler bumming about the dance because he was maybe going to . . . ask me to be his date?

Oh no. I wanted to drop-kick myself down the hall.

Was there any way to take back what I just said? Going to the dance with Tyler would change everything. I wanted to cry: "Wait, wait! I didn't mean *that* dance!"

But then I remembered that small detail about us getting suspended. Suspended. Suspended.

Okay, maybe the dance had dropped down on my priority list.

These thoughts were infecting my brain as Tyler banged on his locker. It was stuck. He banged it again and it still didn't open. Finally he yanked on the lock and punched the locker at the same time, and it clunked open. A book fell out. He bent to pick it up, and something else clattered out of his locker.

Something long and silver. And it had a funky

smell. Was that a . . . ? It was. A big fat *purple* marker.

Tyler picked it up and quickly shoved it into his backpack.

The fact that we were suspended vanished from my mind. There was just one thought there now. A big fat ugly one.

Tyler was the Crusher!

CHAPTER 17

Mild-Mannered Grandmother Pile-Drives Principal!

I WAS SO shocked I couldn't even push the hair out of my eyes.

"That about does it," Tyler said, slamming his locker and looking at me. "Casey? Hel-lo?"

"Oh, me?" I said, tugging on that hair. "Just thinking . . . about . . . everything, I guess." I turned to start walking back to the admin office.

Slowly we walked past rows of brown lockers. Past the Crusher's latest handiwork. Past *Tyler's* latest handiwork?

But even though the evidence was stacked against him, I refused to believe that Tyler would destroy school property. He knew that the Crusher was making the protest harder. He knew right from wrong.

Didn't he?

I wanted to ask him. Straight up. I wanted to grab his shoulders and shake him really hard and ask him to explain the purple marker that had fallen out of his locker. Why? Why?

Back in the admin office, Ms. Kiegel, office manager and chief tyrant, eyed us cautiously. "Your mother is on her way, Tyler. And your grandmother, Casey. Have a seat," she said, pointing to a hard bench across from the counter. The Bench of Shame.

Tyler and I sat in silence. We waited and watched as teachers and administrators handed off papers and joked about the weather.

My forecast: heavy thunder and lightning for the next two days.

The clock above the door ticked so loudly, I felt like I was getting hypnotized. I just kept hearing in my mind: *Tyler is the Crusher. . . . Tyler is the Crusher. . . .*

Finally, Gram strode in. But she didn't look like a grandma in a writing bathrobe today. She was in her city duds. A sharp-looking black blazer. A pencil-thin gray skirt. A white silk shirt. Even pearls. Gram, the professional career woman. I felt another wave of nerves dip my stomach to China. Had I let her down?

She looked me square in the eyes and raised an eyebrow. I raised an eyebrow back. Then she told Ms. Kiegel who she was. Which made the principal appear almost instantly.

"Mrs. Smith, I'm sorry you had to come down here," Ms. Nachman said, as Gram and I walked into her office. "Perhaps you'll have a word with Casey so that we don't ever have to repeat this scene."

"Actually," Gram said, taking a seat and leaning back in the chair, "I was hoping to have a word with you."

The door closed behind her and the three of us were alone.

"Oh?" Ms. Nachman asked.

I was so nervous, I could barely breathe. Actually, Ms. Nachman didn't seem to be lapping up a whole lot of oxygen, either.

"Yes," Gram said, staring at her hard. It was a new view of my sparkly-eyed, teasing Gram. The woman facing Ms. Nachman was made of steel, like a well-dressed cannon. She was ready to attack with logic and reason. Her eyes flashed as she launched the first offensive.

"Ms. Nachman, I appreciate your concern over the vandal, but you are abusing your authority and taking this out on the wrong kids. And I can't let you do that," she said.

I thought of Tyler and quickly looked at the ground.

"Casey was involved in a legitimate protest. She broke no school rules. She's wearing a handmade necklace, and I believe your orders were no T-shirts."

"Yes, but Mrs. Smith, you don't seem to—"

"I *seem* to recall hearing about a cola contract with this school that has not been mentioned at one PTA meeting," Gram interrupted. "You may need scapegoats for your Crush deal. That's obvious. But if you think for a minute that Casey Smith is your puppet in all of this, you will see me at the next school-board meeting. In fact, I might even start researching advertising and marketing in schools. There might be a story in it for *Newsweek*."

I sat there staring at Gram like she had just grown a second head. I knew she was a killer reporter. I mean, I'd heard the stories from my dad about how she'd bulldozed senators and CEOs and even a U.S. president or two. But I had never actually seen her in action. I wanted to jump into her lap, hold on tight and enjoy the ride.

"Mrs. Smith, I beg to differ." Ms. Nachman looked surprised. "Because of Casey's actions, my students are at risk."

"At risk of what? Making fashion statements? Asserting their freedom? Asserting their First Amendment rights?" Gram made a *pfft* noise. "Casey and her friend were not putting anyone at risk. They were taking a peaceful stand against something they think is wrong. They shouldn't be punished. They should be applauded."

"No, Mrs. Smith, y-you don't understand," Ms. Nachman stuttered. "There was a serious act of vandalism here today, and I had to—"

"You had to suspend Casey because she was the student who was protesting this Crush deal in a by-the-rules, positive way. Or is she being accused of vandalism?"

"No! I never thought that she—"

"Then why is she being punished?" Gram demanded.

"Because . . . you're not . . ." Ms. Nachman took a deep breath. She was losing, and she knew it.

"*Perspective,* Ms. Nachman," Gram said crisply. "Two students protest with homemade jewelry and you suspend them?"

"Well, it's more than—"

"Kicked out of school for a peaceful demonstration?" Gram persisted. "Did we learn nothing in the sixties?"

"Perhaps the punishment was too harsh," Ms. Nachman said quickly. "You have brought up some valid points, Mrs. Smith. I'll let Casey and Tyler off with a warning. This time."

Gram raised an eyebrow and nodded. "Thank you for your time. I'm sure you'll make every effort to go through the proper channels in regard to this cola contract." She stood and extended her hand across the desk. The principal shook it limply. Talk about defeated! "I look forward to seeing you again at Parent-Teacher Night."

Then Gram turned, shot me a get-your-butt-in-gear look and led the way out the door. Not that I'd planned to stick around in the principal's office.

Gram made a beeline through the admin office, where Tyler was waiting with his mother.

"We're not suspended!" I chirped.

"Ms. Nachman agreed that it was a mistake," Gram said tactfully.

"Well, this is good news after bad," Mrs. McKenzie said, turning to Tyler. "Let's go get the word from Ms. Nachman firsthand."

Tyler's eyes were wide, as if he were in shock. "What happened?" he asked me as Gram started down the hall.

"Let me walk Gram to her car," I said. "I'll find you in the lunchroom, okay?"

He waved, and I took off.

"Gram!" I yelled, catching up to her.

She put her hand up to her lips. "Not in here. Outside."

I hurried alongside her, my Zing necklace clattering. As soon as we felt the sun on our faces, her fierceness was gone. She was just Gram again. I wrapped my arms around her waist and squeezed as tight as I could.

"Ouch!" she complained, moving my necklace away from her. "That's quite a weapon."

"Oops, sorry," I said. "Gram, thanks so much. I thought that was the end of my middle-school reporting career for sure. You were awesome!"

"Get out!" she teased.

"No really. What would I do without you?"

"Oh, I don't know. You'd forget the number of the pizza delivery place, I suppose. And you'd probably brush your hair before you left for school."

"Gram, you're the best. I hope I can shake up important people like you when I'm a big-time reporter."

"Oh, kid, you know I'll always go to the mat for you." She rattled my necklace and smiled. "As long as you're doing the right thing," she added. "And you are."

Princess Perky Begins Operation Backstab!

AFTER GRAM LEFT, I headed toward my locker to dump out the bricks in my backpack. I was stuffing my reporter's notebook into my pack when Gary's list fell out. The list of people who had access to the coach's office.

Scanning it quickly, I hit the one name I didn't want to see.

Tyler McKenzie.

Of course, I knew he had gym during the period when the equipment room was open. He could have easily cut the logos out of those uniforms.

And then there was that big fat purple marker. Was it the same marker used to scrawl graffiti all over the school?

Was Tyler the Crusher? Could it be true?

I had to confront him.

I marched toward the lunchroom, thinking there had to be an explanation for that purple pen. Maybe he was working on an art project—a sketch of a superhero who wore purple tights?

Get real.

I scanned the lunchroom with no luck. So I headed back toward Tyler's locker. Turning into a corridor, I spotted him. He was at the end of the hall talking to Megan. She was smiling. He was smiling. What was with the smilefest?

"Tyler!" I called out, but he was too far away to hear me. Then I saw him playfully punch Megan's shoulder and turn to go. By the time I got to the end of the hallway, he was gone.

"Did Tyler say where he was going?" I asked Megan.

"Hi, Casey. I'm fine. And how are you?"

"Just tell me where he went, Megan. Please," I said. "It's really important."

"I have no idea." Megan tucked a hair under her rhinestone headband.

"Did he tell you that we both got suspended this morning?" I asked. I was looking forward to her reaction on this one.

"No, he didn't mention that," she said, as if we were talking about the weather.

"Didn't mention it?" I was surprised. "But it was a big deal! A huge deal." And did he happen to mention that he is the Crusher? I wanted to add.

"If you're suspended, why are you still here?" Megan asked.

I put my hands on my hips. "Forget about that. Just tell me what Tyler did say."

"Just . . . something." She looked at me blankly. Like one of those dolls with the face painted on.

"What?" I asked impatiently.

"What what?"

"*What* was he asking you?" This conversation was one for the hair salon.

Megan squared her shoulders and hugged her lavender notebook. "Well, if you must know, he asked me to the dance."

I stared at her. "The *dance* dance?"

"Yeah, the dance dance," she said casually. "Is there another one I should know about?"

I felt like she was speaking Japanese. Tyler? Asking Megan to the dance? Was this day one big bad dream?

"Casey?" Megan said. "Why were you suspended?"

I heard the words but they didn't register.

"Why were you suspended from school?" Megan repeated. "Earth to Casey. Come in, Casey—"

"Oh. I'll, uh . . . I'll tell you later. I have to go," I sputtered. Then I turned to get out of there before flies started landing in my open mouth.

"Casey?" Megan's voice floated after me down the hall.

But nothing made it through the cloud around me. Tyler and the Sugarplum Fairy together at the dance? Wasn't it just about two hours ago he was hinting about going with me?

If only Megan knew that she was going to the dance with the suspected Crusher.

Dazed, I walked outside. The sun was blinding. I squinted at all the students hanging out.

I kept walking, but it didn't help shake off the awful feeling. There I was, fresh from defeating Ms. Nachman—or, at least, watching Gram defeat her. I was still wearing my Zing necklace, still fighting the good fight to keep my school advertising and marketing free. So why did I feel like someone had just kicked me in the guts?

I'm Casey Smith. I have more important things to think about than boys and dances. I have to report the news and save schools and forests and whales and kids and . . .

"Oh, sorry!" I bumped right into some girl. I shook my head, then finger-combed my hair. Wake up, Casey. It was my lunch period, but I wasn't hungry. I decided go to the *Real News* office to get some work done.

When I walked in, I found Ringo lying on Dalmatian Station, staring at the ceiling.

"Ringo?" I poked him. "What's up, bud?"

"Exactly eighty-seven," he said.

"Huh?"

"That's what's up. Up on the ceiling. Exactly eighty-seven tiles. There should be more, but some are missing."

I looked up. He must have been counting for a while.

"Sort of like ceiling scales," he went on. "I wonder why people don't grow scales instead of skin."

I climbed up onto the table and lay down next to him. It occurred to me that I had barely talked to Ringo this week.

"Everything okay?" he asked.

"I guess. If you don't count that I just got suspended, then unsuspended, for voicing my opinion." As I spoke, I counted points off on one hand. "And then there's the fact that Tyler McKenzie might be the Crusher. And if that's not weird enough, we can add Melody to the list. She has a purple marker. The motive. And she suspicously disappeared. Add on the dance insanity that's hit everyone I know, and I'd have to say, it hasn't been a fun week."

"Whoa. So we're in the same mood."

"Really? So why are you bummed?" I hadn't noticed how stained the ceiling was.

"I'm not telling you," he grumbled. "You'll make fun of me, and I'm feeling thin-skinned. I could use some scales right now."

"Ringo, believe me." I sighed. "I'm a mess right now. The last thing I'm going to do is make fun of anyone."

"What's the first thing you're going to do?"

"What? Oh, Ringo! Just tell me what's wrong, already."

He was quiet for a moment. "Well, I gave Samantha my Simon cartoon. The one asking her to the dance."

I pulled myself up on one elbow. "What did she say?"

His eyes shifted to the side, away from me, as if he were a little embarrassed. "She said, 'Nice stationery.'"

"Oh, Ringo." I lay down on my back again, feeling sorry for him. I knew exactly how he felt. Not that I thought Samantha was worth it. But you can't tell Ringo not to like the girl because she's not the sharpest pencil in the box. "That rah-rah wouldn't know a good thing if it slid down her megaphone and she gagged on it."

He shrugged. "It's okay. If she can't dig Simon, then she can't dig me."

"That's the spirit." I kicked at his sandal with my Converse. "I'm sorry. The whole world is one big gigantic mess. A big, messy dance, sponsored by Crush Cola."

He propped himself up on his elbow and looked at me for a long minute. "Right now you look exactly like my aunt Theresa after she eats spicy food," he said. "Her eyes water. Her face gets red. And she swears her lips are swelling shut."

If only my lips had swollen shut over the past week, every time I mocked the dance in front of Tyler.

"Uncle Sam refuses to take her out for Thai. Mexican is out of the question. But the weird part is, she loves the stuff."

Great. Now I'd been dumped *and* I looked like a walking chile pepper.

"Have you been dipping into the jalapeños?" Ringo asked.

"No!" I said, laughing. "Stop that. We're depressed. Remember?"

He lay back down and sighed. "Yeah, I remember. So what are you going to do about this Crusher thing? Set a trap? Call the National Guard? Sing the national anthem?"

"Right now, I need to confront the suspects. Both Tyler and Melody. But Melody is sick. And I just went after Tyler but got sort of . . . derailed."

"I can help you out with Melody," he said. "She lives near me. I'll head over to her house after school and pin her down on this Crusher thing."

"Great! But do you think she'll be honest with you?"

"Hey, I have a sixth sense. Sort of like my aunt Theresa."

"Thanks, bud."

"There's just one other thing. About the dance." He sat up and faced me. "I still really want to go. But I don't have anyone to go with."

"I was thinking the same thing," I said. Out loud. Whoops!

"You?" Ringo poked me. "I thought you thought the dance was stupid."

"Well." I grimaced. "I just figure, I'm a reporter. I should, you know, experience these things. Just so I can write about them. Gram always says you shouldn't limit your experience."

"That's it!" Ringo jumped off the table.

I sat up. "What's it?"

"We can go together," he said. "Me and you. Bud dates."

I scratched at a mosquito bite on my arm and thought about it. Was Ringo serious? Was Ringo ever serious? Could I really show up at the dance after trashing it so much?

Did I really want to go?

Duh. Yeah.

I straightened up and extended my hand for a shake. "Okay, it's a done deal." He shook my hand, then did a back flip right there between the tables.

I hated to admit it, but I was getting psyched. Going with Ringo solved this whole dance problem. I was still bugged out about Tyler and Megan. And I was really stumped by the possibility that Tyler or Melody might be the Crusher. But at least now I felt like I'd cracked the dance code. I was in.

I slid off the table and joined Ringo's celebration dance.

Then a stack of fashion magazines on Megan's desk caught my eye, and it hit me.

I had a problem. The kind of problem I'd never come up against in all my eleven years. A problem that sat like a giant question mark in my brain.

What was I going to wear?

Mall Queens Dethroned— Royal Family Outraged!

AFTER THE FINAL bell rang, I plopped down on the front steps of the school and whipped out my reporter's notebook. My day had been a tornado and I needed to ungunk my brain.

TO DO:

Finish researching advertising in school

on net

Write school sponsorship story

Finish square root homework

FIND CRUSHER!

FIND SOMETHING TO WEAR TO A

DANCE!!!!!!!

I slammed my notebook shut. The thought that Tyler could be the Crusher was too much for my brain at the moment.

I'd been looking for him since lunch, but Kee-Kee Kelleher told me that his mom had signed him out of school early. Something about a doctor's appointment. My plan was to call him as soon as I got home and nail him down about this Crusher thing. And if Ringo was going to interrogate Melody, it looked like my investigation was finally moving along.

Meanwhile I bounced down to the next big item on my list. A getup for the dance. I opened my notebook, and listed the clothes in my closet:

Converse hightops (8 pairs, 8 colors)

T-shirts

jeans, jeans, jeans

denim overalls

That about covered the Casey Smith wardrobe.

Not that there wasn't a lot to choose from at the Abbington Mall, an oasis of shiny floors, mirrors, bright lights and waxy plants. But I had to go. Today. Even I knew better than to wear overalls to a dance.

Luckily, money wasn't a problem. My parents had given me a credit card before they left, for "reasonable expenses." I knew this qualified. And getting to the mall was no big deal. I could walk there. But the place makes me dizzy. If the cranked up air-conditioning doesn't get you, the elevator music will.

I ducked into a department store, home of perfume ladies who travel in clouds of cloying smells. Dodging the stink, I rode the escalator up to the preteen section.

Where I was totally lost.

I had no clue where to start. How do you swim to the surface in such a deep sea of clothes? I flicked through one rack, gingerly touching the hangers like they were about to sizzle the skin off my fingers.

"What about this one?" I heard a high-pitched voice say.

"Cute, but do they have two?" came another mousey voice.

"I don't know, let's check," said the first girl.

I knew that voice. I knew both those voices. Oh, no. It couldn't be. I turned slowly and groaned.

The Kelleher twins. Red-headed twin night-mares not five feet away from me. Their arms were loaded with dresses, and their fire-haired dad trailed behind them, looking more drowned than a cat in the rain.

"Hey, girls, how about this one?" he asked, holding up an old-fashioned, bright pink dress with a stiff lace collar. Even I knew he was holding the goofiest dress on the floor.

"Barforama!" Keely grimaced.

"Dad," Kendall complained. "Don't try to pick stuff out, okay? You should just go sit somewhere and let us do the shopping."

They headed into the dressing room, leaving their poor bored dad behind. Then he turned and saw me.

"Hi, there!" he said, a little too chipper. "You go to Trumbull with my girls, don't you?"

"Uh, yeah," I said. Oh, great. What do you say to the father of the two most annoying girls you ever met? "Yes, I have a class with your nitwit daughters! Boy, do they get on my nerves! You must be very proud about how obnoxious they turned out!"

"I thought I saw you the other morning when I dropped the girls off," he said, smiling.

"Yeah," I managed to say. Poor guy. He seemed nice enough.

"Well, you look as out of place here as I do," he chuckled.

Was I that obvious?

"I'm not big on shopping," I admitted, looking around for my escape.

"Me neither," he said rocking back in his loafers a little. "Usually my wife takes care of stuff like this, but she's been working around the clock lately. She's trying to land a big account for her ad agency. She's got focus groups, meetings in Boston with marketing managers—"

"DA-HAAAD!" Two voices chimed in.

The Twit Twins were standing in identical daisy dresses. They rolled their eyes. "Casey doesn't care about all that," Keely said, tugging his arm.

"Hey, um, I'll see you guys later." I yanked a dress off the rack and backed away like a thief.

"Casey, are you really going to try that dress on?" Keely asked, curiously. I looked at the dress in my hand as if it got there by magic. It was cough-medicine red.

"Oh, this?" I held it up. "No, I just like the color and didn't, you know, want to forget," I lied.

"Well, it certainly is a color, isn't it, Kendall?"

"Yeah, Kee-Kee. It's a color, all right." They were looking at me like I had spinach in my teeth.

I headed toward a different rack and pulled out another dress. I held it up and inspected it, wondering if it was cute or if I only liked it because it was denim like all my jeans.

"Oh, how lovely," Keely sang from behind me. "Look, Casey's going to be a rodeo star."

Kendall snickered. "And when she's done riding wild bulls, she can reupholster her couch." They fell over each other, giggling.

Oh, forget it! I wasn't about to stand there and take abuse from a couple of salt-and-pepper shakers with an attitude problem.

Bolting out of there, I stuck the two dresses on a random rack and spotted the shoe department. That meant only one thing: chairs. Lots and lots of chairs.

I found an empty corner and collapsed in a vinyl chair. Keely and Kendall had only added to my Abbington Mall freakout.

I sat there for a while, watching the people move about like ants under bright lights. If only I had magic powers. Or a fairy godmother. I'd just wiggle my nose and voilà! Instant dress for Casey. Not too frilly, not too rodeo. Something I could live with.

Talk about hopeless. And clueless. And, darn it, still dressless.

I looked at the ugly men's shoes on the shelf by my chair and said out loud to the little tassels: "This is worse than detention."

"Excuse me?"

I tore my eyes away from the tassels. I saw orange shoes. Toni's orange shoes. Connected to Toni. "Why are you talking to those dorky loafers, Casey?"

I sat up and looked at her. How was I supposed to explain that one?

"Girl, you're really getting weird on me lately," she said, smacking her gum. "What's your drama?"

I looked at her funny midriff shirt and noticed that she had an innie belly button. Usually I was on my guard with Toni and just stayed out of her way. But I was so out of my element that I surrendered.

"I'm going to the dance," I blurted. I was waiting for her to bust out laughing. She didn't. "And I can't find anything to wear."

"Well, girlfriend, there's only one thing you can do," she said, moving her backpack from her right shoulder to her left. "Follow me."

"Where are we going?" I asked.

"We're in a mall, aren't we? We're going shopping," she told me as we maneuvered past mannequins.

I had no choice. I had to listen to her. Because first of all, you don't argue with Toni Velez. And second of all, you don't argue with Toni Velez.

"But what about—"

"Don't worry," she said firmly. "Just put yourself in my hands."

Put myself in her hands, huh? I looked at her aqua fingernails and felt a wave of my usual mall nausea.

But this time I didn't know if it was the store's fluorescent lights . . .

Or a bad case of Dance Flu.

Mysterious Asparagus Sparks Meatball Surprise!

"GRAM!" I YELLED as I came through the door. "Come see! I actually got a dress!" I turned the bag over and dumped my stuff on the floor.

I had phoned her from the mall, so she knew that I was going to the dance. Still, I think she was surprised to see me with a big shopping bag.

She stared at the pile of fabric and tissue paper. "Who are you, and what have you done with my granddaughter?"

I laughed. "I'm going with Ringo. Turns out the girl he likes has a pom-pom for a brain."

"That would make for a headache," she said. "Let's see this magnificent piece of fashion."

I reached through the tissue paper, then I stood up and held the dress up to my shoulders. It was ivory, with a barely-there red-and-gold

189

pattern that reminded me of a shirt my mother had brought back from one of her trips. There were tiny shoulder straps. Spaghetti straps, Toni called them. Which reminded me that I was hungry. I'd barely eaten lunch.

"Very elegant," Gram said. "But casual."

"And best of all, it's short. No long, clinging princess gown for me."

"I think it's perfect, too." Gram rubbed the meshy fabric between two fingers. "What shoes will you wear?"

"That was the hard part," I said, picking through the pile to get to my new shoes. "Shoes for girls are so gross. But Toni swore I could wear these black lace-up boots, then hike in them after the dance. My kind of dancin' shoes."

"Really?" Gram nodded. "It was nice of Toni to help you like that."

"I know! She's my lifesaver." I started stuffing everything back into the bag. "For a minute I was worried that Toni would push me toward some teeny-weeny skinny dress. But she didn't try to dress me like a Toni clone. She kept asking me questions like what did I like about this dress, what did I like about that one. Finally we came up with this one. She said the gold pattern played up the gold flecks in my eyes. I didn't even know I had gold flecks, let alone that they're something to play up."

"Does this mean you'll be spending more time at the mall?" Gram asked.

"No way. I am officially finished with all of this dance stuff for the day—and on the journalism clock," I said, grabbing my new clothes and heading up the stairs. "I've got some calls to make."

"Well that's a relief," Gram said. "Make sure you give me all your receipts. And I know you, so I'm going to be a grandma and tell you to hang up that dress. Oh, and we're having spaghetti and meatballs for dinner. How does that sound?"

"Awesome," I hollered, hugging the bag against my closet. "I'll meet you in the kitchen in an hour."

I kicked off my hightops and grabbed the phone. I had to confront Tyler about the purple marker. He had given me his number the other night, and I tried to ignore the fluttering in my stomach as I punched it in and waited. And waited. Finally, the answering machine kicked in. Feeling like a goon, I left a message for Tyler to call me and quickly hung up.

Was it too early to call Ringo? I punched in his number, but his mother said he was still at Melody's house. More waiting.

Then I flicked on my computer, sat down, and started an update for Griffin.

TO: Thebeast
FROM: Wordpainter
   Weirdness of weirds, Tyler might be the Crusher! And even more bizarro, he asked that pink elf Megan to the dance. Don't ask me what happened to her crush, Spence the Politician. He's probably going with another eighth grader who supports Crush Cola. Traitors. And, drum roll please: I'm going to the dance! I know, I know. I'm going with Ringo. His crush inhaled too much hair spray or something so he was left with me. Finding a dress at the mall nearly killed me. But I survived to write this e-mail, didn't I?

I debated telling him all about getting suspended and Gram slaying the Nachman dragon. But then I thought I'd better save it for later. I had to get to work on my story. I hit Send, then logged on to the Internet.

As expected, I found even more information on marketing in public schools. As far as I could tell, the first problem was soft-drink contracts. They almost always led to more and more companies invading a school. Candy companies. Sports equipment makers. Fast food vendors. They were creeping into schools across the country.

There was also something here I hadn't considered: schools in poor neighborhoods. They desperately needed extra money. But sponsorship was more of a problem for them.

Since name-brand sodas and candies are more expensive, kids who are on federal meal plans are out of luck. Some schools allow companies to bring the goods in anyway for computers or textbooks. But believe it or not, lots of schools in poor neighborhoods flat-out refuse the contracts, even though they need the money. Mainly because it causes another rift between students who can afford the stuff and students who can't.

I sat there for a minute and thought about what it would be like to go to a school that couldn't afford a computer center or good library or up-to-date books.

Or a school newspaper.

Were these contracts good for those schools? Or was sponsorship just the easy way out? This was a lot more complicated than I'd realized.

"Casey! Dinner!" Gram called me from the kitchen.

I logged off and headed downstairs.

"How's your story going?" Gram asked, pouring me a big glass of milk.

"Slower than I want," I answered, flopping into my chair. I was starving, and I didn't want to talk about Crush Cola and lose my appetite. And anyway there was something else I wanted to ask Gram.

"Hey, Gram?" I said, pushing a whole meatball into my mouth. "How come pople turn insuch dorks round dime of ig dinze?"

"That was the most unattractive thing I've seen all day," Gram said.

I chewed and swallowed and took a drink of milk. "Sorry. What I said was, how come people turn into such dorks around the time of a big dance?"

She twirled her pasta. "Are your friends still suffering from First Dance Flu?"

"Worse. It's the Pre-Dance Trance," I said. "Everyone's falling for the wrong person. Everyone's going to the dance with the wrong person. Everyone's unhappy."

"Hmm." Gram chewed and listened.

"Pretty ridiculous, huh?"

"Actually, I was just remembering myself at your age," Gram said.

"Oh, don't tell me," I groaned. "You were one of them?"

"There was this boy," she said. "What was his name? David? Dave? Davey! He was organizing a campus canned-food drive, and he had this curl in the front of his hair that made him look just like a younger version of Robert Redford."

"Who?" I said.

"A famous actor," she said, resting her chin in her hand. "Anyway, Davey came to dinner one night because his parents were friends with my parents. And we were having asparagus. The plate came to me, and I gave myself a huge portion, and then I passed it to him. And he said, 'No, no thank you, I don't care for asparagus.'"

"Gram, so he didn't like asparagus," I said. "So what?"

"Well, I always loved asparagus up until then," Gram said. "But when he said that, I looked down at my plate. And all of a sudden, those skinny green stalks didn't look so appetizing. I began noticing all sorts of yucky things about them. They were stringy, and they smelled sort of funny."

"The same asparagus?"

"The same asparagus," she said. "I didn't touch a single stalk of it. Just because Davey didn't care for it."

"Gram, that's ridiculous," I said.

"Casey, I know. That's just my point," she said, raising an eyebrow. "Crushes are like that. They make you go a little bit crazy. They make your brain misfire. They make you do dumb things. You suddenly get interested in ice hockey. Or you develop a liking for peanut butter ice cream. You want to be like the person you've got a crush on. And you want to share things."

"I think I get it," I said.

"Good," Gram said. "Sometimes this weird morphing we do is great. You might discover that you actually like hockey or that peanut butter ice cream is delicious. But sometimes it goes too far, and you can lose yourself. It takes a little time to figure out how to like someone without losing your step."

"It sounds like you needed a thump on the head," I said.

"Maybe I did." Gram chuckled. "But this is just part of life, Casey. It happens to everyone, at one time or another. So you might want to cut your friends some slack. Because it will happen to you, too."

I wrinkled my nose at her.

"It will," she insisted, shaking a forkful of meatball at me. "And when it does, try not to forget how much you like asparagus."

I twirled a long piece of spaghetti around and around on my fork. Gram and her stories. I didn't like asparagus anyway. But I thought I knew what she was getting at. Maybe I was being too hard on Megan. After all, Megan did put the paper first and assigned me the editorial. The editorial that started the whole school thinking twice about Crush.

And what about Tyler? I saw that purple marker fall out of his locker, plain as day. If it had been anybody else I would have laid right into him. But I didn't with Tyler because I didn't want to make him mad. And I was thinking about the dance. The big important dance.

I guess I really did understand this whole asparagus thing. But meatballs are more my style. And no way would I give up meatballs for Tyler because . . .

Wait. Meatballs.

Meatballs?

"Meatballs!" I yelled. "Meatballs, Gram!"

"Yes, Casey?"

"Meatballs are the key!"

"Really?" Even at moments like these, Gram is cool as a cucumber.

"Excuse me!" I jumped up from the table and sprinted upstairs. All these questions that I didn't even realize were tickling my brain started coming to light. I grabbed my notebook and started scribbling like a maniac.

QUESTION: How did Kendall and Keely know that the wednesday surprise lunch was going to be giant meatballs?

ANSWER: They knew because they were in the cafeteria, breaking the Crush Cola machines while Mrs. Stekol was preparing the Thursday "lunch surprise."

Q: Why didn't they want their dad to tell me that their mom is in advertising?

A: Because . . . because they were the ones who "secretly" supplied the Zing shirts. Maybe their mom worked on an account for Zing?

Q: Are Kendall and Keely the Crusher?

As I wrote, more pieces fell in place. Keely was talking about focus groups and market research the day before the protest. When I asked her about it, she said she had read about it somewhere. But at the mall Mr. Kelleher told me his wife was chasing after some big account, doing focus groups and so on. And he said she had her own agency!

I pulled Gary's list out and ran my finger down the column of names. Yup, yup, yup! They were there. The Kelleher twins had gym class at the same time that the supply room was unlocked. The evidence against them was stacking up.

I logged back on to the Internet and found a trade magazine for the advertising field. Then I did a search for Zing Cola. When I saw their headquarters were in Boston, I knew I was getting warmer. Mr. Kelleher said Mrs. Kelleher was traveling in Boston that week.

I found a recent article that talked about how Zing Cola hadn't signed with an advertising agency yet and that big players were bidding for their business. The feeding frenzy had reached fever pitch, the article said. And, hel-lo! Among the agencies competing for this valuable company's business was a new agency with a growing reputation. The name: Kelleher and Crane.

Kelleher, huh?

As in Kendall and Keely Kelleher.

I rubbed my palms together and hit Print. Tomorrow I would be armed with one scathing school sponsorship story for the front page of *Real News*. Plus hard-core evidence against the Crusher.

I couldn't wait to talk to Tyler. So why hadn't he called?

Crusher Busted!

FRIDAY MORNING. TRUMBULL corridor. I spotted Tyler and cornered him.

"Hey, Casey," he said, with that smile of his. The smile that would melt chocolate. But I was an ice cube.

"Get over here," I ordered him, yanking him into a corner. "All right, Tyler McKenzie! Did you break all your fingers? Or did some spaceship land in your backyard and tear out the phone lines?"

"Huh?"

"Why didn't you call me back last night?"

He blinked. "I was at the movies with my dad. You called me?"

"We have a few things to go over. Like, I know that you got the Zing T-shirts from Keely and Kendall Kelleher."

"I didn't tell you that!" he said, holding up his hands.

"You didn't have to," I said, wagging my finger at him like my mother does to me when I wear clothes off my floor. "I did a little digging on my own and found out that their mom is trying to get the Zing account for her ad agency. That's why I didn't recognize the logo on the shirts. It was a prototype—a new logo that she had designed for the new account."

"It was supposed to be a secret," Tyler said, lowering his voice.

"Because their mom gave them the shirts?" I asked.

"Actually, no," Tyler admitted. "The twins swiped the shirts. They said the cartons were just sitting around in their garage. Their mom still doesn't know they're gone. And she could get in big trouble if the Crush people found out. It would look like she was deliberately trying to sabotage them because she wanted to work for Zing."

"So they were protecting their mom?" I asked him. "Or do they think they were protecting her? Do they really think if Crush loses one sponsorship that it's going to increase the sale of Zing? Talk about small minds."

He gave me a confused look. "What are you talking about?"

"I'm talking about the fact that the twins are the Crusher." I stared at him. He just stared back. "Maybe they didn't want anyone to know they were supplying the T-shirts because that would brand them as anti-Crush. They had to seem neutral so no one would suspect they were the ones vandalizing the Crush campaign."

"Kendall and Keely?" Tyler said, looking down the hall. "I don't know, Casey. That seems like kind of a stretch. I mean, do you have any evidence?"

"I have some facts that point to them," I said. Then I swallowed hard. "But there is one bit of evidence that doesn't really seem to fit. And it's about you."

Tyler put both hands in his pockets and pulled his shoulders back. "What?"

"I saw that purple marker fall out of your locker yesterday," I said sternly. "What's up with that?"

Tyler shook his head. "I'm not the Crusher, but I think you might be right about the twins. The purple marker—it's Keely's. I borrowed it from her to make some anti-Crush signs."

I was so relieved Tyler wasn't the Crusher that I nearly cracked up. "You goon!" I said, pushing him back a step. "I seriously thought it was you until last night when I was eating meatballs."

"Meatballs?" he said, tilting his head. "What

does that have to do with—"

"Hi, ya, Tyler," Keely sang from a few lockers away. She and Kendall sported big cheese-eating grins as they sauntered over.

"Hey, guys," Tyler said, taking a step back.

"My sister and I were at the mall last night, you know," Keely said, eyeing him like a cat. "We got some great outfits for the dance. Do you, uh, know who you're going with yet?"

Tyler stared her down. "I'm going with Megan O'Connor," he said quietly.

Ouch. It hurt to hear him say it.

"What?" All the charm drained out of Keely. Her simpering smile disappeared. Now she just looked like an angry carrot. "You're taking Megan to the dance? Not me? After all I *did* for you!?"

"What *have* you done for him?" I demanded sharply.

Keely glared at me and took a step backward.

"Nothing!" she spat. "I mean, I just meant that I, you know, I helped him. That's all I meant."

"Nice try," I said, folding my arms. "I know you gave Tyler the shirts for the protest. I also know you were in the cafeteria when the vending machines were vandalized. How else would you know that meatballs were the Wednesday surprise lunch? You knew because you were spying on Mrs. Stekol to make sure the coast was clear."

Keely and Kendall looked at each other, then back at me.

I had them right where I wanted them.

"That's stupid," Keely said with pinched lips. "Why would we want to vandalize anything?"

"Because your mom needs the Zing account," I said, taking a step closer to the criminal duo. "You lied when I asked how you knew about focus groups because you didn't want anyone to know your mom was in advertising. But she is. And you've been trying to sabotage the Crush sponsorship, thinking . . . what? If the deal is nixed, Crush sales will drop? Do you have any idea how piddly the profits from our school would be compared to the millions those companies make?"

"That's the dumbest thing I ever heard," Kendall interrupted, standing in front of her sister.

"Really?" I asked. "Then what were you doing with that purple marker—the one that Tyler borrowed?"

They stared at me like a dog who's just been busted digging in the garbage.

"Admit it," I said sharply. "You hated Crush because your mom needs the Zing account. So you took action. Vandalizing action." I stepped up on Keely. We were practically nose to nose. "You and your sister are the Crusher. It all adds up. Square root *that*."

Keely looked back and forth from my left eye to my right like she was taking an eye exam. I could hear her heavy breathing. But I didn't back down. I stood my ground, waiting for her to cave and blurt a confession.

Which she did. Sort of.

"You . . . don't . . . understand!" Keely started wailing. Fat tears rolled down her cheeks.

Kendall was crying too, standing right behind Keely with her hand on her shoulder. "Our mom needs to get this Zing account so she can afford to send us to a private school!"

"If she doesn't get it, we don't get to move to Boston!" Keely whined.

Kendall's slender nose was turning red. "Is that so wrong? Boston is so much more fun than this stupid town."

Tyler stared at the bawling twins as if they were lobotomized frogs.

I, on the other hand, was not surprised at all. The K-twins had never struck me as being overly concerned about the rest of us in this school. Part of me was burning mad at them for being so selfish. The other half, the kinder Casey, felt sorry for them. They just didn't get that there was a whole huge world out there with other people whose lives were touched by their stupid actions.

"So you think vandalizing school property was the answer to your problem? All because you want to go to private school?" I was so mad, I felt like I could chew through a tire.

"Well, um . . ." Keely was a vision of puffy eyes. "Kendall dared me to jam the machines, so I did. Then it was her turn, so I dared her to mess with the uniforms. And then it seemed so easy. So we wrote all over the walls. Maybe it got out of hand and, well—"

"Well, *what*?" I demanded.

She sobbed even louder. "I was really just trying to help Tyler!" She lunged forward and grabbed Tyler's arm.

His eyes bugged out of his head, and he pulled away. "Thanks but no thanks," he said, wiping his sleeve as if she'd left mud marks.

I wanted to cheer, but I bit it back.

"I swear, you guys!" Kendall pleaded. "Zing told our mom that if Crush stole any more of their market, they would cut their advertising budget. She'll lose the account! We didn't mean to get you in trouble, Tyler."

"Tyler, you have to believe me. We wanted to help *you*!" Keely whined. "You seemed to hate Crush so much. I thought if I took the dare and broke the machines, you'd be happy."

"Happy?" Tyler said. "You made everyone who was anti-Crush look like a criminal! Casey and I almost got suspended because of your so-called help. That kind of favor I don't need."

He took Keely by the arm. I guess he figured Kendall would follow like a duck on her way to the pond. "We're going for a little walk to Ms. Nachman's office," he said, taking charge.

Keely's face went white. Even her freckles looked pale.

"Ty-ler!" she whined. "Are you turning me in? I can't believe it!"

"Believe it," he said without looking at her. Then he looked at me and winked.

I was still mad at the double-twits, but if there was one thing in the world that could distract me right now, it was that crooked tooth.

We marched to Ms. Nachman's office like a fast-moving funeral procession. When we walked through the glass-front door of the administration office, Tyler stopped and let go of Keely's arm.

"You figured the whole thing out, Casey," he said, resting a hand on my shoulder. "You do the honors."

Ms. Nachman walked to the counter and folded her arms. "What is it now, Ms. Smith?"

I stepped between Kendall and Keely and put my arms around their shoulders like we were three best buds. Then I smiled my biggest grin. "Allow me to introduce you to . . . the Crusher."

Girl Reporter Kicks Butt!

"The *Kelleher* twins?" Megan gasped.

"Double your trouble, double your headache," I told her, flipping my backpack onto Dalmatian Station.

We were in the *Real News* office for a lunchtime meeting. The school was buzzing with the news that the Crusher had been caught. But I had the full scoop. As usual.

"Man, that is so wild," Gary said. "You have to admit they did a good job of camouflaging themselves from suspicion."

"They seem so sweet," Megan said, staring into space and smoothing the blue velvet cuffs of her shirt. "I mean, they always dress so cute."

"What can I say?" I sat down and swung my green Converses onto the table. "Sometimes criminals come in matching minis and sweater sets."

"So what was the damage?" Toni wanted to know. "Did you find out what the punishment was?"

"That was another roadblock," I said, pushing back the brim of my cap. "Ms. Nachman took them in her office and shut the door, so I couldn't listen in. But then during math I figured out that I could maybe convince Ms. Nachman to tell me their punishment since I would most likely"—I looked at Megan and raised an eyebrow—"since I would most likely be writing a story for *Real News* to show kids what can happen when you mess with the system."

Megan looked at me. Silence.

"This is the perfect story to run side by side with my school sponsorship piece," I said matter-of-factly.

"Maybe." Megan gave in. "Did you get the info?"

I looked around like a cat who caught the canary.

"Signed, sealed and delivered!" I said, waving everyone to come closer to hear the juice. "Okay, first of all, they get two weeks' suspension."

"Two weeks?" Gary said. "Starting today?"

"And they miss the dance," I said. "Plus, they

have to spend their weekend scrubbing graffiti off the walls."

"Nasty!" Toni declared, wrinkling her nose.

I rubbed my hands together like a villain. "And there's more. They have to pay for the cost of the vandalized machines. Except not with money. They have to work off the debt by slinging hash in the cafeteria with Mrs. Stekol!"

"Eeeww!" Megan pretended to shiver. "Do you think they'll have to wear those creepy hair nets?"

"If they do, I'm sure they'll be matching ones," I said. "I wonder if that's in fashion at private schools?"

Megan giggled, then touched my arm. "Casey, stop! Let's not be mean."

I blinked. "They almost get me suspended, and I'm being mean?"

Just then, Mr. Baxter stepped into the doorway. One hand held a stack of textbooks. The other hand clutched a computer printout that I recognized. My story.

"Good work, Casey," he said, his beefy face lit by a wide grin. "I have to apologize. I was wrong to reel you in on that editorial." He nodded toward the admin office. "The powers that be haven't been thrilled with all the attention on the Crush deal, but you were right. And you've done a fabulous piece here. *And* you nailed the Crusher. Good for you!"

"I can't figure out why they'd do such a thing," Gary said. "I mean, why were they so anti-Crush?"

I gave everyone a quick rundown of their mom's ad agency, and how they thought they were helping out. "They figured if they screwed up the Crush deal here at Trumbull, other schools might follow. And since Zing is Crush Cola's biggest competitor, Zing stands to gain. And with profits up, Zing would hire the Kellehers' mother to do their advertising."

"Sounds way complicated," Toni said. "Bottom line, those girls just wanted their sorry butts in some preppy Boston school."

"They made some bad choices," Mr. Baxter said.

"And they'll pay the price," Megan said, pulling herself back into editor mode. "But that reminds me. Your article on corporate sponsorship was really good. I read it as soon as you gave it to me this morning."

"Thanks." I kicked my feet back up on the table, trying to look like I wasn't at all thrilled.

"Good work, guys!" Mr. Baxter said again. Then, as quickly as he'd appeared, he vanished.

"I mean it," Megan went on singing my praises. "I'm impressed. I thought your anti-Crush feelings would come through, but you told both sides. And that stuff about those poor schools really touches a nerve. So I'm running it on the front page for next week. Oh, and if you can get the Kelleher Crusher story to me by two o'clock, I think we should run that, too."

"See, Megan?" I said, putting my hands behind my head and reclining just a bit. "You're not all lip gloss and denim collars."

"Ha ha, Casey," she said sticking her tongue out at me. "I also showed your sponsorship story to Spencer, along with the poll results. After I added them up it turned out that seventy-three percent of the students said they should have been informed about this deal from the beginning. Spencer took that seriously, Casey. He talked to Ms. Nachman this morning."

Was it my imagination or was this day totally unlike my last two weeks? My story approved. Both stories. The Kelleher twins getting busted. Megan agreeing with me. Was this some weird fifth dimension? Did I have food poisoning or something?

"Now I hate to say I told you so, but I will. Because Spence is *so* a good guy," Megan said, beaming. Glowing. Okay, she was blinding me. "He's proposing that we keep the Crush logo on our team uniforms and scoreboards. That'll give the school some money for the things we really need, like the science equipment. But everything will be debated in the next SGA meeting. Then it will be presented to the PTA."

"Any talk about getting us new computers with the money?" I asked.

Megan rolled her eyes. "Get real. But the point is, you did it, Casey. You gave our school its power back."

"Wow," I said, smoothing my hair behind my ears. "That's almost better than having a front-page story." Almost.

"Better than a front-page story?" Ringo said, trudging into the office. "What's better than a front-page story for Casey Smith?"

"What happened to you, Ringo?" I asked. "You look like you slept in your clothes."

"Well, I didn't sleep in these," he said, plopping in a chair. "But only because I didn't sleep. Well, not much."

"What?" Megan asked. "Why not?"

"I stopped by to see Melody after school yesterday. To scope out whether or not she was the Crusher," he said. "Her flu turned out to be just a twenty-four-hour bug, so she was feeling better. But she was totally bummed because she didn't get to make her sculpture. You know, the one the art teacher was going to display at the dance?"

I suddenly remembered thinking that Melody was the Crusher because I saw all those pens in her satchel. And also because she didn't show up in her Zing necklace yesterday. Talk about feeling guilty. The poor girl was hugging the porcelain all day and I had her pegged as a criminal.

"I remembered it was recycling day, so I scored all these cans," Ringo went on. "You'd be surprised how nice the recycling guy is if you offer to bring him french fries and vinegar instead of ketchup. I tried it. It wasn't bad. Not as good as ketchup but the vinegar is sort of—"

"Ringo! Your point?" I said.

"Oh, right," he said, yawning so big I thought his face was going to stretch off his skull. "I stayed up all night and helped her make the sculpture."

"Ringo!" Megan was touched. "That is so sweet!"

"And so dangerous," Toni pointed out. "Check out your hands, dude. You look like you've been playing patty cake with a chainsaw."

"Injured in the line of duty," Ringo said, inspecting his nicked fingers. "All in the name of art."

"But Ringo," I said, a little baffled. "Wasn't Melody's sculpture an anti-Crush statement?"

"Yeperdoo," Ringo admitted, rubbing crust out of his eyes. "It sort of looks like a weenie-mobile. Like that one at the school that already bit the big sponsorship hot dog. Melody's calling it *Crush the Imperialist Corporate Swine*."

We all laughed. Except Megan.

"And just what will rah-rah gag-me Samantha say?" I asked. "Won't she be peeved at you? She's pro-Crush, remember?"

Ringo shrugged. "Melody needed help. Samantha isn't down with Simon. It seemed like easy math to me. And the last time math was easy was in the fourth grade. Now I have geometry. Who cares where the train is going and how fast it's getting there?"

I gave him a big bear hug. "I was beginning to think your crush on Samantha was affecting your brain."

"Nah. It's just affecting my wardrobe," he said, picking at his purple socks. "My mom says I have to wear fancy clothes and shoes to the dance."

Oh, no. My stomach landed in my hightops.

I know I should be the happiest girl reporter in the free world since everything worked out so great. And I did feel satisfied that the science department would get new equipment and the students would get to vote on the Crush deal.

But that didn't change the fact that I still had one last scary hurdle in front of me.

The dance.

Students Bop till They Drop

THE FLASHING LIGHT lit my bedroom.

"No cameras!" I ordered. "Gram, put that down or I'll erase your hard drive."

"Very funny," Gram said, pointing the camera at me and snapping a couple of pictures. "I'm more scared of what your parents will do if I don't get this on film."

I groaned and held up my hands. "Pictures of what? Casey in a dress? It's just like a big T-shirt, but longer."

"Gotcha," Gram said, putting away the camera. Then the doorbell rang. "I'll get that." She passed by, patting me on the shoulder. "You look wonderful," she called on her way down the stairs.

I stepped in front of the mirror. I don't know

about wonderful. But I had to admit it felt great to be all dressed up . . . and still *feel* like me.

I clomped down the stairs to find Ringo standing in the foyer, holding a bouquet of . . . cabbage?

"I thought you would think flowers were too girly," he said, handing me the leafy ball. "This seemed more like you."

"Uh . . . thanks, I think," I said. "That's thoughtful."

Gram eyed the cabbage as if it were a precious heirloom. "Next time, bring us some asparagus," she told Ringo.

"You look so . . . fancy-schmancy, Ringo," I said. He was completely un-Ringo, in a starched white shirt, black blazer and black pants.

"Don't worry, I'm still Ringo," he said, pulling back the jacket to reveal tie-dye-patterned suspenders. "And check out the footwear."

I glanced down. Sure enough, sticking out below his fancy pants were bright purple socks and Birkenstocks.

"Mom and I compromised. I told her that strangled feet cannot dance."

"And she understood?"

"Blames my dad. She says he's allergic to shoes, too. Hey, you're not allergic to cabbage, are you?"

"Absolutely not," I said, grabbing the fat bouquet. "You ready?"

He pointed toward the door. "Your Volvo awaits. Actually, my dad's Volvo awaits. With my dad inside. Hey, you're wearing boots. Are you allergic to shoes, too?"

"Let's go," I said, lugging him out the door.

"Life is a dance. Some just dance slower than others."

The theme was "A Night in New York," and I had to admit that someone had done a good job covering up the stinky, echo-chamber gym. Cardboard skyscrapers hid most of the folded-up bleachers. I waved at Mrs. Stekol, who was in charge of the NY DELI booth. That woman loves to feed us. Gary and Natalie, his swimmer friend, were waiting in line for drinks at the MANHATTAN WATERWORKS booth. And nowhere was there a sign for Crush or Tasty Weenies or Crispy Fries. I was happy to see that the dance was totally ad-free.

One cardboard building was marked MUSEUM. It featured Melody and Ringo's sculpture proudly displayed at the top of a set of bleachers. The lights were low, and a mirrored ball made glimmering patterns fly along the floor.

The rest of the room was filled with kids dancing to loud music in what was supposed to be Central Park.

It was sort of exciting. Sort of sweet. And not so scary after all. "Ringo, let's go see your sculpture over—"

"Hey, you!" Megan interrupted me. "We've been waiting for you guys to show!" She was dressed in pink from head to toe. A slim silky dress, which was okay, I guess. But she carried a tiny handbag with pink beads all over it. Not too practical. The thing was only big enough to hold about half a tissue.

Then she stepped aside, and my heart gave a little dip.

There stood Tyler, all tall and dreamy and so cute my knees wobbled for a second. He wore a brown jacket over a navy shirt. And his hair was combed back in this wave that sort of emphasized his dark eyes. I'm telling you, the guy could melt chocolate with one look.

I touched my hair and smoothed my skirt.

"Is that a dance move?" Ringo asked me.

I ignored him.

"Hey, Casey," Tyler said.

"Hey," I said, unable to stop staring at him. "So, um, did you hear Ms. Nachman's announcement in seventh period?" I asked quickly. "She said that because of the poll results, she was going to tell the Crush people that we needed time to decide what to do as a school. We're going to have an SGA and a PTA meeting to talk about it."

"It's all over the school," Megan answered. "And it's great, Casey. But don't you ever want to leave *Real News* behind and just have fun? This is a dance!"

"I think the announcement was awesome," Tyler said, poking me in the shoulder. "But I wish Nachman had just told Crush to take a hike."

A week ago, I would have agreed with Tyler. But I'd learned a thing or two since then. Which I began to tell him, in full Casey motormouth mode. "Well maybe she still will. The important thing is that at least the students will have a say. And maybe the science department will get the equipment it needs. Is that worth the price of our teams' wearing the Crush logo on their uniforms and—"

"Hey, I have an idea." Megan interrupted. "Why don't you two dance while you discuss this?"

"Want to?" Tyler asked me.

Was I dreaming? "Me? Sure. I'm . . . yeah." I wanted to smack myself. Had my lips been seized by alien invaders? But why wasn't he dancing with Megan?

Tyler and I started weaving around kids at the edge of the dance floor and—*whooosh!*—the song wound down like a deflating balloon.

"Let's slow things down for a minute," the deejay announced. A sweet ballad began, like a funeral song. Kiss of death for a middle-school dance. Suddenly, the dance floor emptied out.

We both stopped in our tracks.

"Do you want to wait till—" he began.

"Definitely," I said. No way was I going to be Casey Smith, girl reporter, in a slow dance display.

As we backed away, I spotted Megan dancing with Spencer the Politician.

"Look at that," I said. "The editor of the school newspaper dancing with the head of the SGA. What a power couple."

"I think he was supposed to come to the

dance with Kendall Kelleher," Tyler said. "Guess that didn't work out, huh?"

I grinned. "'Politician Caught With Crusher's Better Half.' That could get him bounced out of office for sure."

Tyler went for soda—a variety of choices, I might add—while I headed off to the girls' room. Skirting around a clump of cheerleaders, I went into a stall and shut the door.

"I just don't get it," one of them said. "Ringo was mooning around me all week. I thought for sure he was going to ask me to the dance. But he never did."

Wait. There was only one Ringo. And there was only one girl he was drooling over all week. I peeked through the crack in the door. Sure enough, it was Samantha.

"He was practically your *slave*!" one of her friends chimed in. "Would you have said yes?"

"Sure." Samantha shrugged. "He's cute and cuddly, like a teddy bear. I kept waiting for the big question. Do you think I should have asked him?"

They kept chattering as they left the girls' room. I emerged from my stall and faced myself in the mirror. Something was fishy. Ringo *did* ask her to the dance. He told me so. I mean, was she so rah-rah clueless that she didn't know the

Simon cartoon was an invitation? Or . . .

Wait a minute.

I hurried out of the bathroom and scanned the gym, looking for Ringo. I finally spotted him, hanging outside the MUSEUM with Melody. I made a beeline across the floor.

"Hey, Melody," I said.

"Casey!" she cheered. "Congratulations on your story. Ringo told me all about Crush getting the sack!"

"And your sculpture looks . . . really interesting," I said. "Hey, could I borrow Ringo for a second?"

"Sure, right right!" She gave me a squeeze and headed for the NY DELI. "All right, buddy," I said, backing Ringo into a corner. "Spill the beans. How come I just heard Samantha complaining in the bathroom about how you never asked her to the dance?"

"Beans are a wonder food," he said. "Loaded with protein. It's nature's perfect, tiny pellet of—"

"Come on, bean boy. I'm waiting."

Ringo fidgeted with his suspenders. "I . . . just lost my nerve," he said, shifting his gaze away from me. "I was embarrassed to tell you."

"Oh, really?" I said. I wasn't buying that sorry excuse for a minute. "Ringo, you never asked Samantha. Megan comes with Tyler, but dances with Spence. And pushes me to dance with Tyler. What is going on here?"

"Nothing. Not a thing," Ringo sputtered. "Except that we knew you wanted to come to the dance. So I decided to ask you to come with me."

"But . . . what about Samantha?" I demanded.

"What about her?"

"She's the girl of your dreams!" I said, shaking him by the shoulders. "I may not like Sam, but I'm not you. Why would you go with me if you could go with hypoglycemic, Diet Cool–drinking Samantha?"

"Don't get mad, Casey. I mean, I'm sort of off Sam. And I'm not supposed to even say anything about the plan. Not a word. Toni and Megan will kill me."

"Toni's in on it too?" I asked.

He nodded. "And Gary. But my lips are sealed." His gray eyes were serious. He wasn't going to budge.

"Okay, don't spill. Let me guess. Megan came with Tyler just so she could get him to the dance."

Ringo nodded.

"But how did she know that he even wanted to come?"

"You can thank Gary for that. He got the four-one-one from Tyler, who wanted to ask you, but wouldn't because you kept putting down the dance so much."

I knew it. Me and my mouth!

"And Toni," I said, thinking aloud. "Toni at the mall. That was no accident. She followed me there to play fashion consultant?"

Again, Ringo nodded. His head was beginning to remind me of a bobbing buoy.

"So you guys were behind all of this," I said aloud. My friends had snowed me. *Me*. I didn't know if I should be grateful or mad that they had meddled.

"You people," I started to complain. "I have never seen such a bunch of nosy, interfering—"

I felt a hand on my elbow. Tyler's hand. Connected to Tyler.

"The music's back," he said, grabbing my hand. "Let's dance."

Melody was right behind him. "Ooh, I quite love this song," she singsonged. "Ringo, may I have this dance?"

"What are you gonna do with it?" Ringo asked in his usual Planet Jupiter way. They tangoed dramatically to the dance floor.

Tyler put his arm around my shoulders and led me into the boogie fray. Before I knew it, all of us were dancing together. Gary with his swimmer girl, Toni with some groovy dude, Ringo with Melody, Megan with Spencer.

And with me? Tyler.

"This is just so great!" Megan beamed. "I knew it would all work out!"

The deejay switched to a fast, funky song that I loved, and Tyler screamed something in my ear. So I screamed "What?" back in his ear. And he yelled in my ear again. Finally, we just looked at each other, and at the same time we yelled, "I can't hear you!"

So of course we both blurted, "Jinx!" and socked each other in the arm. I couldn't help but giggle. Then he grabbed me and did this crazy disco move that made me dizzy. Dancing is not my favorite thing in the world, but you won't get a complaint out of me.

Are there better ways to spend a Friday night? Get real.

My Word
by Linda Ellerbee

MY NAME IS LINDA ELLERBEE. Parts of the Casey character are based on me: I am a journalist. As an eleven-year-old girl, I was shy *and* had a big mouth. One covered the other. But not very well. In this book, the part about Casey making fun of the dance and then being heartbroken not to be asked—well, that part actually happened to me. The ending was different. That's all I'll say about that.

However, there are in this book, as in your world, issues besides dances and boys. (Are they *as* important? Depends on when you ask, doesn't it?)

Take commercialism in schools. This did not happen when I was a kid. But that was then. Today schools all across the country are facing questions raised in this book. Truth is, sometimes schools don't have enough money for stuff that might be considered "extra," such as new sports uniforms or an art class—or new computers for the school paper! So if a big company offers to buy these things for the school, and all the school must do is agree to sell or advertise the big company's product at school, what's wrong with that?

Tricky question.

We live in a commercial world. Many of the TV shows we like would never be made if there weren't commercials to pay the bills. Our favorite magazines wouldn't exist without advertising. Same with newspapers. Even our clothes often come with some company logo or designer's name printed on the outside, which is just another kind of advertising, isn't it? The good news is: Commercials are not acts of the devil (although many are truly boring). So what is bad about a company wanting to advertise *in* school?

Maybe nothing at all. But then, maybe . . .

You tell me.

Is it an age thing, I wonder? Is the world saying to you: "You're young. You will be unduly influenced by commercials. You won't understand that when someone is trying to sell you something, first they try to make you think you *need* the thing they're trying to sell you. We have to protect you from the real world. You can't do your own thinking yet. When you're grown, you can watch all the commercials you want."

I hope it's not that. I'd like to think adults had more respect for kids' intelligence.

But there *are* some pretty good reasons for not filling your school with commercials. Casey states the case pretty well; it's really about price. If you think something is wrong, are you willing to stay quiet, or would you be willing to rattle your world a little? *Silence* about what you believe can be costly. What's your price?

Of course, making a noise can be expensive, too. Especially if you want someone to ask you to that dance.

I don't have an easy answer, because there aren't any. Often it's hard enough just to figure out the right questions. "What is *your* price?" is a good question. But not the only one.

As I said, it's not easy being a kid today.

Or a parent.

Or a teacher.

Okay, so it's a big, loud, confusing new world, but it's yours. Truly, it is. So if you don't like it, go change it. Be a one-girl revolution. Get up and do something.

Get real.